T0079936

THE SHADOW-BOXING WOMAN

THE GERMAN LIST

THE SHADOW-BOXING WOMAN

Inka Parei

TRANSLATED BY KATY DERBYSHIRE

LONDON NEW YORK CALCUTTA

This publication was supported by a grant
from the Goethe-Institut India

Seagull Books, 2018

Inka Parei, *Die Schattenboxerin*
© Schöffling & Co., Verlagsbuchhandlung GmbH,
Frankfurt am Main 1999

First published in English translation by Seagull Books, 2011
English translation © Katy Derbyshire, 2011

ISBN   978 0 8574 2 591 1

British Library Cataloguing-in-Publication Data
A catalogue record for this book is available
from the British Library

Typeset by Seagull Books, Calcutta, India
Printed at Trio Process, Calcutta

She's my neighbour. We've been living on the same floor for years. Every now and then, we insert our heavy keys into the Prussian doors in sync. Then I disappear into my hallway, a long, narrow tunnel lined with yellow hemp carpet, barely three feet wide. And she into hers, with the floorboards still painted the standard 1940s' brown. The paint is hideous. Emitting a matt sheen and almost impossible to remove, it resembles the excrement the German Shepherds deposit on the pavements here, fed on rust-coloured lumps of pre-processed food.

For a week now, it has been silent in the side wing of the formerly elegant Jewish apartment house on Lehniner Strasse, of which she and I are the only residents. A wing of gloomy rooms typical of Berlin's architecture, shaped like rectangles with one corner chopped off, rooms with three external walls, practically impossible to heat, with shared toilets half a floor down.

The last few remaining tenants moved out before the winter began, most of them to the vicinity of some relative or other, into the concrete tower blocks with central heating and waste disposal units out in Marzahn or Hellersdorf. The last to leave was a bedraggled old woman who lived halfway down to the basement. For twenty years she had refused to leave her quarters. Semi-blind, her ulcerous legs wrapped in floral-patterned rags, she was taken to a home in early November.

I'm sure now that I'm alone in the building. I've been the only one to trigger the roars of our shared cistern for days; my neighbour isn't here any more. No jangling of keys, no coughing, no other people's footsteps to be heard any more. Occasionally, a gust of wind catches the door to the back yard and slams it shut. Otherwise all is quiet, quiet as a stone. Only the sound of my footsteps echoes off the splintering glazed tiles of the entrance area. I pull up the hood of my anorak, shoulder a bundle of plastic bags and enter the yard. Armed with a long hooked pole, I plan to get rid of the past week's trash. Since the last dustmen turned up here in the summer and took away the old iron trashcans, this has been a procedure that calls for special tools and a degree of dexterity not to be underestimated. Late mornings are ideal, when the people in the neighbouring building are at work and not staring out of their windows in disapproval.

I step up to the wire fence put up above the low brick wall since the reintroduction of private property, dividing their premises from ours. Cautiously, I push the pole through a fist-sized hole until the hook grabs the plastic handle of the trash container, and open the lid by lowering my end of the pole abruptly. Then I have to throw the plumply tied, pale green bags up in the air so that they fall down at an acute angle on the other side of the wire, landing in the opening if possible, or at least near to it.

I spend several minutes throwing bags over the fence and correcting their position. Then I turn around, reaching for a bag of deposit bottles behind me. And suddenly I see the sign.

It wasn't there yesterday.

It's screwed to the grey-scabbed wall smeared with graffiti and wet briquette ash. A shiny new sign, the sign of a construction company. A name and address are framed below a blue enamelled symbol of a house.

I lean against the fence and close my eyes, breathing wet winter air and imagining the wall bare. Then I open my eyes again. The sign is still there.

It was unlikely they would just forget this ramshackle building while all the others are being done up one after another. It was predictable that I wouldn't be able to hide out here forever, without a rent contract, unknown and unregistered by any public body. But why does the last official resident have to vanish at this very moment, the woman called Dunkel across the hall, my outside toilet partner? She's left me alone, now of all times. After not being away for long once over the last couple of years, not even for one or two days.

I can see her before me, balancing shopping bags slowly upward along the remainders of the banisters, pushing her forearms ahead. A cautious person, presumably closely attached to particular places. She never has visitors. I can't recall ever hearing the sound of her doorbell. Only the tiny rituals of loners: putting her black lace-up boots next to the doormat in the hallway with the toes pointing outward, always on the left, and on the right the ash bucket (I do it the other way around). Snapping the safety chain and the lock shut loudly between eight and nine in the evening when she doesn't go out, and sometimes briefly opening the door beforehand and closing it loudly again, to make sure she's bolted out the feeling of night seeping in from the cool of the staircase.

Without thinking a great deal about her, I assumed that the circle she drew around her life consisted of her 370-square-foot draughty but almost rent-free dwelling, the shared staircase, our streets around Rosenthaler Platz and a few necessary contacts in other parts of town. Her being simply gone puts me off balance.

To add to that, I've been surrounded for days by nocturnal creatures, by woodlice, cockroaches and small rats, all disputing my right to live here. And I recently made the mistake of exploring the deserted front part of the building. Now the cream-coloured upholstered suites rotting on the ground floor loom over me in my dreams at night, sniffing at a blue shirt from the communist youth organization, petrified with dirt, that was hanging from a window frame on the second floor. It has grown into my skin at the collar; I can't take it off. To be brief—my nerves are shot.

From the remains of a gutter hanging steeply from the roof, melted snow drips onto my skull, running down behind my ears to the back of my neck. I raise my head and look up to the top floor. After a week's thirst, the fern in Dunkel's kitchen is already yellowing at its tips. I stand on tiptoe. Why didn't she at least ask me to water her plants? Through the grease-smeared window-pane, I see the blurred contours of a pack of salt, a carton of milk printed blue and white and a loaf of bread, which I envisage already coated with green fur on the cut edge.

My eyes wander over to the next window. Did something just move behind the glass? Shocked, I drop the bottles and look around. I take a run-up, swing onto the carpet-beating frame and climb onto the second, man-high wall that closes off the yard. Blue-green shadows flicker through Dunkel's living room like flames, underlain by the slightly audible bass blanket of a newsreader starting in and breaking off to the rhythm of the pictures. And now the lights go on in the kitchen, the main room and the larder. No doubt about it—the hand touching the switch must be soundless, fleshless. It must belong to an entity that can go a week without heating, does not empty its bowels and has my neighbour on its conscience.

With a clatter of glass, I flee out onto the street with my deposit bottles.

In Mirca's cafe, seated before peppermint tea and potato soup, I manage to calm down a little. Mirca, a pale Romanian with black hair, grins at me and pushes an ashtray across the table. I tamp my tobacco into my pipe and lean back in the armchair in my favourite corner, from where I can view the entire cafe and a wet grey section of Weinbergsweg.

Out on the street, three ragged Roma children are pushing and shoving over a yellow plastic watch they have fished out of a chewing gum machine, a gambling den for kids. They insert two-mark pieces, and the metal octopus with tiny casings on the end of its tentacles circles but usually only grasps a globe of sugar and food colouring. A boy of about eight sneaks up behind them and grabs the prize out of their hands. As the girls leap away with jerky movements, their joints stiff with cold under thin skirts, he stuffs his booty into the shaft of his rubber boot. His scar-ridden mouth opens into a grin, baring gold teeth. There is a twitch in the remains of his nose, ripped ragged by civil war, as the boy skips out of my field of vision.

Not much is going on in the cafe at this time of day. A hipster sipping milk and honey in orange leather pants and an apple-green knitted top is the only customer aside from me. My friend Mirca brings milky coffee. With awkward, trembling movements, he balances the steaming bowl over to the edge of my table.

You can't expect waiterly elegance from a penniless painter who has to act the proprietor to feed his family. A staircase next to the bar leads down to the cellar, down to Mirca's gallery, to his large-format nightmares of Ceausescu's regime. People on cold Stalinist boulevards, with doughy faces and the necks of oxen, as if terror were a hormone that distorted growth, children's heads behind the window of a home, no necks, no bodies, piled on top of one another like cabbages. Those climbing back up the staircase have a brief paleness about their faces, strongly resembling Mirca's. No one has ever bought a picture, nor do I know anyone who has been down there a second time.

My attempt to summon up information about Dunkel fails miserably; I've never been interested enough in her. Perhaps it's because women like her and me are ten a penny in this city.

Once, the spring before last, I stood outside the door to her flat. I looked for the handle on the wrong side, feeling I was acting out a familiar movement back to front. As if I suddenly had to write with my left hand. I was clutching post addressed to her, which the post-man had accidentally delivered to me—perhaps confused by our names. Her name means dark, my name means light. As she stood in the doorway and looked at me, we both flinched. We've been living next door to each other for years but we had never come so close to one another. Feeling as if I were looking into an uncontrollable mirror, I pressed the envelopes into her hand and scuttled back into my hall as fast as possible.

I'm going to break into Dunkel's flat once I get back to the side wing. After years of hard training with Wang a couple of blocks away from here, opening the lock should be no problem. Calling the police is out of the question; it's not as if I were a legal tenant in Lehniner Strasse. And you never know whether they'll bring dogs. Wang doesn't just teach students punches and kicks but also the 36 Chinese Survival Stratagems. Wang has taught me how to wait, calling it a feeling for the right moment. So I wait. Curling smoke is my pacifier and chronometer for Strategy No. 4: Leisurely await the laboured.

For the second time in as many days, I've made the mistake of picking up the wrong tobacco pouch, absent-mindedly smoking hot French tobacco instead of Oriental with a kick of vanilla. Disgusted, I throw my pipe onto the table, staring it down like an evil goblin about to leap upon me. And really—an ugly face I wanted to forget for good forms anew out of blue fumes, creeping out of the smoke like a genie from a bottle and gazing at me.

I'm walking down the street again, on a spring day in 1989. I'm back in my old, now absolutely unreal, life on the city's western axis. As yet, I don't know anything else. As yet, I don't have the impression that this life was a deception, risky and carefree. Lived at the cost of today's life, a life for which I can barely summon up the energy some days.

It's a hot day, too hot for spring. The streets of Kreuzberg around Görlitzer Station shimmer with heat and sand. The sand blows over from the remains of the station, a neglected vacant lot riddled with pairs of train tracks. Capped by the Wall, the line lost its purpose decades ago, now reverting to desert and steppe.

It's late in the afternoon. The area is beginning to fill up. Mid-range cars packed to the roof with Turkish families are looking for parking spaces. People get out, slamming the doors, lugging tired children and the remains of their family barbecues into entranceways still cold from winter. A little girl with blackened front teeth looks down from almost all the house fronts; the picture is fraying at the edges, corrugated by poster glue. Shouldering a stick in a paramilitary stance, she confronts passers-by with her speech bubble: Join the Revolutionary First of May.

Small groups already broken off from the end of the rally are approaching from Lausitzer Platz, walking toward me apparently unhurried, in no rush at all. The only telltale sign of tension is the way they unswervingly stick to one direction. The drivers of the green and white police vans, their windows barred and grated, look bored. They stop now and then to chat, rolling up the sleeves of their ochre-yellow uniform shirts, listening in to snatches of radio messages. On the opposite side of the road, two sixteen-year-olds have tied their red Palestinian scarves around their mouths and noses and are starting to dig cobbles out of the paving around a flowerbed.

There are various options for approaching the probable nucleus. You can turn onto Wiener Strasse from the southeast, coming from Neukölln, and then slowly advance from its green tail end into the dusty part lined with trendy bars lit up like basements and dirty gaming halls and launderettes, which ends at the iron pillars of the raised train line. Here is the strategic centre, which both sides hope to conquer. Or you start on Oranienstrasse, crossing Adalbertstrasse and Mariannenstrasse and once again approaching the overhead train lines, this time from the northwest. The end point of my route is always the kebab shop next to the crater in the ground. Where the supermarket went up in flames this time two years ago.

This year I've decided on the southeasterly approach. As I advance as slowly as possible along the large paving stones, I keep mentally listing the five side streets along which I can turn off and disappear in a flash if things should get dangerous: Glogauer, Liegnitzer, Forster, Ohlauer, Lausitzer Strasse. Side streets leading into calmer territory. You can get to a bus stop from there. Growling and swaying, the yellow double-decker buses approach at regular intervals, driving out of the danger zone along Kottbusser Damm.

A fat man in a brightly printed shirt is securing the barred windows of the Turkish Bank with sheets of wood, plainclothes police in jeans and sports jackets dividing the greasy strips of plastic at the exit of a pizza place. From a distance, Caribbean drumming echoes through the hemmed-in streets. Block by block, I push my way through the crowds. The pavements are tightly packed with dreadlocks, badly fitting suits, the synthetic material of black headscarves shimmering in the heat, the rough, poorly circulated hands of street-fighters, festering nose rings and bare white calves above bulky boots. I'm almost at my destination. Only Lausitzer Strasse separates me from the Ankara Grill, where they already put out enough plastic chairs at lunchtime to cover the area between the doorway and the cycle path, so they can hand out kebab and warm bottles of beer to all the people standing around.

Behind two figures with woollen hats over their faces and petrol canisters, I go to cross the street. There's a screech of brakes as a column of vehicles turns the corner. The doors open before they even come to a halt. Green-armoured figures leap onto the street and form a row in front of me, a row of plastic heads, chest protectors and raised shields. Alongside me, a panic run sets in in the opposite direction, tearing me along with it.

If only I'd stayed put.

The only sentence in the weeks afterwards, murmured over and over, alone, my eyes widened in shock, tearless and dry, and the bitter-tasting mouthpieces of cooled pipes. But I don't stay put. I drift along with the others across the street, stumble through a bush and clamber up the hill on all fours, onto the grounds of the old station.

At the top of the hill I turn around. The tips of chains of green uniforms are closing up, freeing up the side streets again. Below me, part of the angry crowd has turned around and is beginning to battle its way through to the street, throwing stones. If only I'd brought along a stool and sat down in a doorway or on the pavement, like the neighbours looking on unmoved.

It's getting dark. I tread on bushels of grass I can't see. There are no streetlamps here. I decide to climb down into the sandy crater, where groups of people are sitting in the glow of distant bonfires surrounded by bongos and empty bottles. Quiet curses. Nearby, a lighter flickers aflame and I hear a woman's voice.

'I sat like this all night once. Nothing to drink, nothing to eat, crapping in the bushes. But the pigs — they bring their own toilets and set them up by the road.'

A throaty bass adds an agitated: 'Yeah, chemical toilets!'

Then the woman again. 'No kidding, and food. They've got everything they need. Bandages, especially for pigs, and food parcels. Man, the food. Proper dinners and all that.'

'Yeah, with ham and sausages.'

'And chocolate, and biscuits!'

'Wine, champagne!'

Backsides and feet in coarse leather dig into the slope. They laugh, dropping down and rolling to the bottom as I hasten along at a less steep point, cold, finally sitting down on a little hill of sand and pulling my dress down over my knees until it rips. Now I'm beginning to see the point of the leather armour I saw people sweating in at midday.

And then the dog shows up.

It's huge and dark brown, and it's not on a leash, just a crumpled scarf slung around its neck. It has separated off from a pack of snapping knots of fur, heading toward me. Its flanks move in a seemingly clumsy gallop, almost leisurely but very fast.

I look around for help. Little groups emitting hoarse laughs at some distance, turning their backs on me. I jump up and start running, away from the fires, toward the ruins of a railway building. The dog realizes I'm running away. A shudder passes through its body. It pushes up its speed. I've reached the old brick building and walk in, trying to close the half-open rusty door but failing. I'm standing there between puddles and used needles, surrounded by the stench of urine. My hiding place is a trap.

Now my memory, merciful, blacks out for seconds: the dog's leap, snapping for my shoulder, the scream and fall, the growling over me, the smell of flews and fangs, until a shadow moves by the door and a command, hissed in unfamiliar language, removes the wet paws from my chest. I sit up, crawling to the door. With a kick from heavy boots, it falls to.

The light goes on.

Two flashlights fastened to the wall illuminate windowless quarters. I make out wooden crates, a camping table covered in a stained oilcloth, plastic bags and backpacks. Horsehair protrudes from the burst seams of a mattress on the floor. A slight shove at my chest makes me sit down.

Before me crouches some kind of dwarf, swathed in his stinking cloud of smoke, with a stubble of red hair, a rampart of tangled silver earrings, in striped pants and army boots. Over his shoulders the black-encrusted, spray-painted remains of a leather jacket. His head is slightly too large, like that of an embryo. His nose is short, covered in grey freckles. He has eyes with no colour and nicotine craters on his cheeks. A pipe is stuck in the corner of his mouth.

He fetches two bottles out from behind the bed. He leans over to me, handing me one of the bottles. As I reach for it he grabs my ear and tugs it toward him, to his lips. I groan. My beer rolls across the floor. He makes a pincer of his thumb and forefinger and rips out my earring, holding his bloodied trophy under my nose and then pushing me back.

I cower over, sobbing. He looks at me with empty eyes and drinks. Then he begins to talk, his voice harsh, taking no breaths. He sees that I don't understand him, interrupts himself, stands up, walks to and fro, suddenly grinning and declaiming another sentence. Twice, three times. I stare uncomprehendingly and he laughs again. He switches his voice, expression and language, now speaking slowly, almost patiently at my face, speaking in French with a hard accent, words that instantly bring me to my unsteady feet.

'*Ma petite.*' He steps up to me, raising a hand.

'Calm down.' His whisper is a voiceless rasp.

'I'm not going to harm you. I just want to know if my little one understands me.'

4

By the time I leave the cafe it's afternoon. The trams, screeching orange caterpillars made in Hungary, lurch up the tracks toward Prenzlauer Berg, full of school-children and part-time secretaries. I turn the corner, knock the lukewarm pipe against the bullet-ridden facade of Number Fourteen and enter the building. Last year's advertising flyers, rotted to papier mâché, attach themselves to my heel like a bridal train, only releasing me after I brush them off on a bicycle stand with a nervous scrape.

I cross the yard with twelve slow paces, as a breathing exercise, and to warm up I take the four flights of stairs at a run. Outside Dunkel's flat, I bend my knees in a low position and destroy the lock with a side-on kick just below the trim. At the end of the hall, a dusty ray of light falls onto the floorboards from Dunkel's half-open room. The kitchen must be on the right because mine is on the left. The door is closed, a radio playing behind it. Nothing moves. Slowly, I walk toward the light, push the door wide open and leap back into my guard position.

In a semi-circle of chairs placed in the middle of the room, I find the opponent I've been fearing for hours: an arrangement of multiple sockets, extension leads and several time-switches, connected up to the TV, stereo and ceiling lamp.

Like two substances unintentionally stirred and coagulating within me, the tension of the fight and the humour of the moment intermingle. Swaying between laughter and nausea, I reach a window, push the clammy bolt aside and vomit an unappetising version of Mirca's cuisine into the yard, now dripping from the thaw.

I stand there a while, letting the glass cool my forehead and cheeks. I scrape snow from the windowsill, stuffing it into my mouth and then spitting it out again. My head resting on my folded arms, I lose myself gazing at a cat strolling greedily around the garbage containers next door. The aged window glass distends its image, inflating its belly. It's standing on the concrete base of the fence, lifting one front paw in indecision, then it leaves the kink in the window and inserts its head through the half-open lid of a garbage can. The swelling passes through its behind and tail, disappearing as the cat begins to rip open the trash bags.

Dunkel's room is the most cluttered space I have ever seen. With the exception of an empty strip leading from the door to the window, it consists of untold layers of objects piled next to and on top of each other. I stoop and find a newspaper from 1990 plugging a hole in the floor. Like a dense blanket, dust runs along the skirting boards to the posts of a brass bedstead plastered with plump feather duvets, abandoned clothes, books, a tray of teacups, tubes and bottles, crumpled peppermint packets, batteries, a Walkman, cassettes, a torn-open pack of condoms. A flecked, folded silk-painting frame, a limp guitar cover, sheet music, two full ashtrays, several screwdrivers. An overturned vase of lacquer flowers, a pumice stone for smoothing cracked heels, clothes pegs, hairpins, screws, barrettes, a scratched telephone card and false fingernails, surrounded by a layer of grains of sand and breadcrumbs.

Next to me, by the window between hat stands, cardboard boxes and a mountain of kindling made of hacked-up fruit crates, is a small plastic-coated desk, too small for a grown woman. The drawer handles are decorated with flowers of smudged pink nail varnish, the tabletop covered in the advertising stickers that eight-year-olds like to collect. At one corner protrudes a ring binder of notes made by the older Dunkel. I pick it up, flick through it and realize she must have studied French years ago but since decided to let this layer of her life gradually vanish under a sediment of empty chocolate wrappers, scraps of cloth, reminders for unpaid bills and a hill of collected pfennigs coming forth from an upturned tin can.

Cautiously, I put my find back down and bury it again. As I do so, I discover the branded symbol hidden on the desk's rear outer edge, a reddish-brown heart burnt through the plastic onto the wood. At its centre are the small, upright letters *M.M.* There's only one way to make this dusky red sign that looks like it's grown into the material: a candle, matches, pins and a steady hand. Prick your fingertips, hold the pin over the flame and burn the first dot when it starts glowing. Then quickly, before it cools off, press the red juice from a fingertip until it drips into the hot wood. A slow process. The work of many hours, fingers pricked to pieces and dozens of spoilt pins. But the pain of first love imprinted here for eternity heals far more slowly. And sometimes never.

The floorboards behind me creak. Footsteps. In a startled attempt to turn around I knock against a man-high cactus, completely desiccated. Of an indeterminate shade, it must have entered into a camouflage relationship with the curtain behind it over the years. At the last moment, I raise my fists into a block in front of my face and stomach; then the bulky monstrosity rams me, its spikes digging inch-deep into my lower arms.

A man, almost six foot six, leaning against the door, watches me. If he were going to attack he'd be standing differently, more tense. Rather rough-hewn hands with thick silver rings dangle from the bulges of a greasy blue jacket. He has cat-length, sand-coloured hair and sharp creases between his mouth and nose, too deep for some-one of my age. His eyes are incredible, a warm green burning that I have to turn away from immediately, but his mouth, the contemptuous touch around his dry, cracked lips—I don't like that mouth.

Not letting him out of my sight, I push the plant back into the dusty folds of cloth and slowly extricate myself from Dunkel's junk. The man pulls a pack of tobacco out of his pocket, hesitating as if he might be making a mistake. He opens it, finds his papers and pulls one out without looking. Across his eyes, which I can hardly bear, flickers amazement and a diffuse fear, not directly related to me. Now he scrabbles for filters, plucks up tobacco and rolls a cigarette blind, still staring at me. He seems to be waiting for me to make a move, for a word, a gesture, a leap. But doing nothing is one of my strengths. I gradually move into a lower position, the stream of air through my mouth and nose losing its urgency as if I wanted to transfigure myself into a piece of Dunkel's furniture.

A knot of fears untangles itself as my breath flows. Maybe he's from the squat across the road, Number Twenty painted porcine pink and turquoise, which sends out regular troops to look for useful material in ruins and on building sites? Or is this man a friend of Dunkel's, an unsuspecting visitor who thinks I'm a burglar? Does he have something to do with her disappearance?

A tree-brown, stick-thin beast appears before me, like a locust, with long grasping arms pointed heavenward and bent as if in prayer. With the black dots of her two oversized egg-white eyes, the praying mantis stares out from her glass cage, between tarantulas, mealworm beetles and cockroaches. Wang and I are sitting alongside her on a bench. We're waiting for feeding time at seven in the morning, in the insect section of the Berlin Aquarium.

The centrally heated air and the sight of apathetic crocodiles have made me sleepy. Wang taps me on the shoulder. The keeper appears with a trolley of plastic cups. He opens the door to the cage, places a cup inside, removes the lid and shuts the enclosure again. We step up to the glass. A fly crawls out, grown feeble in captivity, flies a brief, lurching circle and lands on a small-leafed shrub next to the mantis. The two of them are absolutely motionless. The mantis has become the dry branch on which she is perched.

'Watch her very closely. She's waiting for the fly to move,' Wang explains. 'If she makes the first move, the fly will see her and flee. But if the fly moves first she can catch it in motion.'

I yawn, trying to keep my mind on the matter at hand. Half an hour passes, neither insect moving. Then I must have turned away for a blink of an eyelid. When I look back again, a shimmering lump of fly is dangling from the grips of the praying mantis, already bitten into.

Wang calls this the origin of Strategy 16: To catch something, first let it go.

And really, the man's starting to squirm. He lights a cigarette, taking a drag that makes the tip glow almost white, blowing smoke into the room out of his mouth and nose. He flicks ash onto his shoe, steps from his left leg to his right leg and back to the left. His eyes glide over me as he smokes the cigarette in a few hot drags. Heat rises to my torso. He drops the cigarette and puts it out with one foot, takes a deep breath and takes half a pace toward me. His voice is surprising, brittle and gentle at the same time.

'You're the neighbour. The woman with the pipe.'

I raise my head in amazement. A cable knotted between two chairs, stretching across the room, grazes the back of my head. The man's eyes flash wide and he jumps straight at me. A moment before he leaps past me, I realize he's not attacking and lower my defences. He grabs at a plug, pulls it out of the socket and comes to a standstill at breathing distance. The dry skin of his arm brushes across my forehead as he fiddles with my hair to release my hair slide.

'Good conductor.'

He laughs, tapping a finger against the copper surface of the barrette dangling from the electrical terminal above us. I'm trembling. My attempt to strengthen my control only makes it worse. I have an inkling of what's going to happen; his right arm is approaching my shoulder. He'll want to embrace me, calm me down. I respond with the snake technique, a fast, extremely underhand dig of my fingertips between two strands of muscle above his armpit.

He doesn't scream but he takes an audible breath. Then he tears his body in another direction, the way you swing around to take a different route because the old one has turned out to be a dead end. He pushes his way to the windows and opens the pane that has slammed shut again. The frame releases clumps of ice with a slurp. With his left arm, he swings himself onto the windowsill, turning his feet outward.

'I saw a cafe round the corner. Come on, we can talk there.'

We set off without another word.

As we're leaving, I take a brief look into Dunkel's kitchen. Greasy wallpaper, a used juicer on an old kitchen dresser, little black pots of withered basil leaves, pots and pans piled in fragile towers on open shelves, the same tiled corner with a coal stove and hobs as in my place, next to it a gas heater shiny with silver stovepipe paint.

The stench of Dunkel's last breakfast hits me. As I'm about to turn away I discover an envelope next to the leftovers, a rectangle printed with a blue house. I breathe in the air I'll need for the short distance to the table and back, take the letter, recognizing Dunkel's address in the envelope window, and put it in the breast pocket of my anorak.

Then I follow the tall blond man into the corridor. He's shouldered a bulging army backpack, and the dry rot-ridden floorboards groan beneath his feet.

5

Mirca raises his brows when he sees me coming, the second time today and in company to boot. He puts a plastic sign bearing the emblem of a brewery and the word 'reserved' over the burn mark on my regular table. A barely noticeable shake of his head indicates that my life is coming off the rails.

Not much later, he appears at the table. He conjures up a pad to note down our order but hasn't got a pen. My companion orders two cognacs.

'You look like her.'

'Like who?' I ask, a superfluous question.

The man opposite me doesn't reply, just looking at me with a gaze far too green. Slowly, his tongue glides out of his chapped lips, wetting a cigarette paper with its brown-stained tip.

'It was a week ago, at that flea market in the Tiergarten.'

Mirca has returned behind his bar and is polishing two non-standard, curved glasses. He takes a bottle off the mirrored spirits shelf, fills two measures into a schnapps glass and pours them into the larger ones.

'Siebzehnter Juni.'

The man at the table looks uncomprehending, until I realize he must be some kind of tourist.

'Seventeenth of June Street,' I explain.

Mirca comes back to the table, two glasses in one hand. He slaps down cardboard beer mats, puts the drinks down and marks the edge of the beer mats with a tally.

'She was working on a hat stall. She was frozen stiff, her heater was broken. I got her a coffee and we talked for a bit. She wanted to show me around town. We met up that evening at Plänterwald.'

His elbows planted on the table, the man grabs his glass. It looks exaggeratedly fragile in his hands. He empties it and swallows, turning the glass in his fingertips.

'Plänterwald?'

He takes his time to answer, making a show of patting his pockets for his lighter. Grinning, he lights his cigarette, leans his head back and closes his eyes, blowing a trail of smoke at the wings of Mirca's ceiling fan. His eyelashes are the colour of fresh straw. The stubble on his chin shimmers in reddish gold. Don't think about it. I feel in my pockets for my pipes and hold them tight until my knuckles start to hurt.

'Here's the south ring. And the east-west line. It runs parallel to the Spree, crosses the south ring and goes on to the suburbs.'

Bending forward, he tips out a box of matches and lays out train lines, apparently determined to prove he knows city. With the map-obsessed ambition of a stranger in town, he points at the thick bundle of tracks cutting the city into north and south on the train map.

'Treptower Park. Plänterwald.'

Pepper and salt slam onto the table, and now I know. I remember a visit to relatives in East Berlin, a morning in a living room in a new block of flats, hours sitting in the plush of a corner sofa, sweat at the backs of my knees, dusty cake and sweet, orange-coloured liqueur. Later we went on an outing, an endless march across green spaces along the river Spree. There was an island and a pleasure park, watery cocoa and a cement-coloured sausage that weaved its way along my imma-ture intestines over three tortuous days.

'We met at the Soviet War Memorial. She was sit-ting on the bottom step of the remembrance hall. The one with the huge stone guy splitting a swastika in two.'

Mirca is folding paper napkins. He fetches a brass-coloured triangular holder from a shelf and tears open a pack of red serviettes. They have to be folded in half to fit in the holder. He folds in full concentration, his head slanted, not looking in our direction. He deliberately

ignores a well-dressed couple at the next table, sitting
behind empty plates and waving their wallets.

'She wanted to take me on the big wheel. We
walked through the whole park and then into the woods.
By the time we'd arrived the thing was closed down for
the night. We sat down on a pile of wood and drank tea
out of a steel flask. She'd brought it along in a big shoulder bag.'

The couple get up and go over to the bar. Mirca
raises his head, smiles unconcernedly into their impatient faces and opens the zip of a wallet fastened to his
belt.

'Then she had the idea with the pedal boat.'

'Pedal boat?'

'There was a boat hire place on the river. The shed
was locked but there were a few boats pulled onto the
bank. We pushed one of them into the water, and then
we pedalled down the Spree.'

'Toward Köpenick?'

The man hesitates, tapping a finger at the bottom
right corner under his matchstick lines. I nod.

'It was two in the morning by now. The area was
totally dark. No lights, no bridges, no houses. Just jet-
black water and industrial buildings with steaming pipes
running along the outer walls. East German industry,
you know.'

'Where are you from?'

'The Rhine-Main region.'

'Where exactly?'

'Near Frankfurt.'

I take my glass in my hand and take a sip, the scent of alcohol tickling my nostrils.

'And then?'

'There was a leak in the damn boat. We were bailing and paddling like crazy to get to the banks. The lower we were in the water, the harder it got to manoeuvre the boat. In the end we got stuck on a landing stage.'

Strange, I just can't imagine my fine-boned neighbour taking a trip in a pedal boat with a strange man in the middle of the night. I could have sworn she was a person who abhors any unnecessary physical exertion.

'We climbed up and sat down on the jetty. Not for long though. It was freezing cold and our clothes were wet. So we set off to look for a bridge, a taxi stand, anything. We spent almost an hour walking through allotments. There was nothing in the area at all, not even a telephone. Miles and miles of garden houses, sheds, fences with pictures of Alsatian dogs.'

Mirca starts collecting up ashtrays. He wanders from one table to the next, piling them on top of one another, a daredevil double row on his lower arm and the palm of his left hand. I can tell by his face that he doesn't care in the slightest whether they fall down, and so he manages to transport the swaying ash-laden towers effortlessly to the bar.

'And Dunkel? Did she know where to go?'

'No more than I did. It took a long time for us to reach a proper road. The worst road I've ever seen. Cobbles patched with tar, covered in weeds and holes and tram tracks leading to nowhere. There were a couple of tenements too. I wouldn't have thought anyone lived there any more, but there were still tenants, I saw flowers on the odd windowsill.'

'With violet neon lights?'

He nods.

Mirca puts new glasses on our table. I can't remember anyone ordering them. The man at my table has fallen silent, looking at me, his eyes forcing mine into their corners. Then he leans back again, lights the next cigarette, taking a deep breath to talk as he raises his shoulders. His words come out in fits and starts. As if something inside him had to shove the sentences to break their way through his harsh vocal chords.

'A bridge took us to a deserted suburban street. And then she collapsed. Threw herself on the dust in front of a huge advertising hoarding and wouldn't take another step. I consoled her, shook her, shouted at her, one after another. It was no use. She simply refused to carry on. Until I saw the green S for the suburban railway. A little sign lit up at the other end of the road. I showed her it, told her we were nearly there. Then she did get up at last. It took ages to get there. Warehouses, chemical factories, an old brewery. An absolute no-man's-land for pedestrians. But she didn't even notice. She dragged herself along next to me in silence, putting one foot in front of the other without looking.'

'What station was it?'

'Schöneweide. By the time we got there the first trains were running again, and the station snack bar was open. Full of people knocking back the first schnapps of the day. The men behind the bar were twins, two tired-looking guys in tracksuit tops. They sold me coffee and greasy French fries in plastic cups. Dunkel shovelled it all down but I couldn't eat a bite. I stood up to go for a pee and when I got back she was gone.'

'Gone? Why was she gone?'

'I don't know. At first I thought she'd just popped out for a minute. But she still wasn't back twenty minutes later. I walked once round the whole station but I couldn't find her. Then I got on the next train.'

'You just left her there all alone. In the middle of the night!'

'It was getting light by then. I was tired. And anyway we had to go in two different directions. She had to come back into town and I had to get to Biesdorf.'

'Is that where you're staying?'

'Yes. Allee der Kosmonauten. In an apartment.'

'What are you doing here?'

A brief twitch of his eyebrows.

'Business trip.'

'Did you want to see Dunkel again?'

'Not really. She's too complicated for me. But still. I wanted to make sure she's OK before I leave.'

'That doesn't seem to be the case.'

I wave at Mirca. He comes over, pulling out his pad. A silver ballpoint pen is wedged behind his ear. The pen with the screw-off tip, just like the day I first entered his cafe.

That was in January.

January in my third winter here, the harshest I can remember. The whole city is caught up in the brace of the cold. There are traces of snow everywhere, on fence posts, the tops of trees and in the gutters. Like today but not thawing, residues freezing stiff for endless days as the temperatures have fallen too low for more snow.

In the front building of Number Fourteen, Lehniner Strasse, a hard core of residents holds on that year, each of them sticking it out for a different reason despite the first cracks in the walls.

Two gay variety artistes live on the third floor with a four-metre-long brown and white spotted boa constrictor. I can see into their back room, which has been converted into a kind of terrarium and must be damp and humid, deteriorating the building's substance even more. I hear them arguing long and often over the great deal of housework their zoo requires. At night I see the glowing openings in their small stove, which has to be fed around the clock. They also keep tarantulas, a parrot and a docile-muzzled black mastiff. The dog follows them like a calf-shaped shadow when they carry their snake basket down the stairs toward the Friedrichstadtpalast theatre every Monday and Thursday.

Opposite them lives a nun from an Indian sect, a subtenant of one of her fellow believers who has gone away to Southeast Asia. When she walks across the yard with her head held high early in the mornings, her orange habit shines like a clear flame amidst the greys and browns of rotting urban substances. Now and then we chat in English. I find out she's actually Jewish and comes from Argentina. Giggling, she tells me about the stains she found under the carpet in her hallway, sniffing with her nose to the floor, the contours of the last tenant but one — a suicide whose putrefying body ruined the paint.

The third flat that is still inhabited is on the ground floor on the right and is the headquarters of a group of mainly homeless alcoholics. Some of them have keys, others ram bottles against the door at night until someone wakes from their alcoholic daze and opens up. The gas and electricity have been cut off; you can see them walking around with flashlights. The actual tenants are a bearded Saxon and his pointy-nosed, swollen-eyed

female companion, half of whose body has strong
shakes. They have a child, about six years old with a
pointy nose of his own. Fortunately, he only has to come
here at weekends. Beneath the bright knitted threads of
his synthetic hat, his face always looks very pale.
Mechanically and reluctantly, he takes pigeon steps
between the childishly swaying adults.

Dunkel is the one I know least about. We greet each
other every day with a silent nod. Now and then our
water pipes freeze up, sending nothing but a thin trickle
of rust to the upper floors. On waterless days like these
she often waits to hear the rattle of my keys in the corridor, only to creep downstairs half a flight behind me,
armed with plastic bottles. Once she reaches the ground
floor she sees me on the stairs to the basement, hurries
down the final steps and lines up behind my knock, taking a deep breath of relief.

There's no point waiting for a reply. I press down
the door handle and we enter the basement flat.
Backyard light shimmers through high windows onto
the bleak chunkiness of 1930s' furnishings. Post-war
wallpaper is mouldering on the walls. The tenant is lying
on her sofa and waves us through into the kitchen.
Sometimes she spoons away at ready meals delivered
daily, or she burrows, her dead husband's glasses bal-
anced on her nose, in a pile of magazines illustrated with
the heads of the European aristocracy. All around her,
the chaos of neglect reigns: cardboard suitcases spilling

over with threadbare material, dust-blind glasses on the lace doilies of a coffin-like chest, mountains of broken household goods and old paper. As we place our canisters in a dirty basin and turn the tap on, I throw occasional glances at my neighbour's expression, recognizing my disgust on her face.

It's the same winter as I begin to live on oats, peanut butter and vitamin tablets, drinking hot water and learning to darn clothes. I've used up almost all my savings.

Often, I sit on a bench on the patch of grass opposite, referred to entirely unjustly as a park. I stare with revulsion at the flanks of the dogs chasing in circles after sticks and salivated balls. Freezing, too lazy to run with their pets, the owners stand around, the dogs' leashes slung around their necks in hangman's knots.

My routine is always the same. Two hours' training in the morning, on an empty stomach. Then a long breakfast and a midday nap, hastened by the high of my past exertions. In the afternoon I take aimless walks around my neighbourhood or walk from Hackescher Markt via Alexanderplatz to the City Library, where they have free newspapers and cheap lemon tea that tastes of vending machines.

When I feel like escaping the city I descend into the tunnel of crumbling orange, from where a train goes north. I always sit by the window in the last carriage. As the train draws into the station I look for the blue suits of the ticket inspectors out of the corner of my eye. The

last stop is Wittenau. From there, I walk until I reach
the little village of Lübars. When the Wall was still
standing, the place served as a substitute for a scrap of
country life for us children. Now it's quiet here. A few
paddocks, a row of houses along a rutted cobbled road
and a village church, several farms. Sometimes my memory takes a leap back to the early 1970s, a four-year-old
holding her father's hand, him carrying a bag of
chopped apples for the horses. I walk and walk, crossing meadows of long grass and frozen streams to the
Tegeler Fließ, the widest stream. As long as I put one
foot in front of the other I can persuade myself I'm doing
something useful.

In the evening I take the suburban train back into
town and work on toughening up my fingertips.
Following Wang's instructions, I ram them hundreds of
times into a pail, the first year filled with rice, then with
sand and later with iron filings. After that I eat my
evening meal, top up the coal briquettes in the stove and
fall into a dreamless sleep.

On an icy, smog-grey morning I take my last twenty-
mark note to the new cafe on Weinbergsweg.

There used to be a shoe shop here. A store bled dry
over years, which I walked past every day and never
saw a single person going in or out of. Behind orange
protective film stood the same pairs of cloven-footed
lace-up shoes, plastic-coated pumps and black patent

children's boots. The old writing above the door, a row of grubby, naively slanted letters, has not been removed, apparently giving the cafe its name.

The place is busy already. Chic freelancers are sitting restless and glutted behind the remains of champagne breakfasts. Three builders pour whiskey into each others' coffee. An old woman is dipping white bread into her stew of pork and beans. And the new landlord, visibly struggling to keep up, is buzzing and reeling between the patrons, his forehead moist.

I head for a corner table, picking up a newspaper from a leather holder on the wall. In a rustling struggle with its paper walls, I wait for my order.

No wonder there are so many people here. It makes sense to be a regular at a cafe where the food seems to be good and cheap, with shiny tables and chairs of freshly oiled wood, and the discreet but not shady light flowing along the walls out of delicate paper fans in metal frames, not neon tubes. At least if it's the only one of its kind on the whole block, in the midst of fast-food, old Berlin-style corner dives and Chinese takeaways dispersing the charm of tinned bamboo.

The door flies open, banging against a rubber stopper mounted on the floorboards to protect the glass from the pointed metal strands of a chaotically shaped steel and brass coat stand.

But it doesn't fall to again; someone holds it open. From outside, a corridor of cold pushes its way across the room, stroking against my feet. I squint over the edge of the paper and make out two figures standing still in the entrance. Wide-legged and unconcerned, they don't close the door with a kick of a heel until they've made eye contact with the landlord, who instantly grows even paler — something I'd have thought impossible. He dumps a tray of dirty glasses he'd intended to take into the kitchen down on the counter.

They stride over to the bar. The taller one, blond and around forty with a backside rendered even fatter by the wallet in his right back pocket, shoves his legs forward, enclosed in chemically bleached jeans and sneakers with large tongues and open laces. The kind you often see teenagers running around in these days. His jacket is lined with fake fur, concealing the plastic grips of Taiwanese flick knives beneath the ends of its sleeves. His partner is slightly smaller and more agile. He has pumped-up biceps, a rank growth of sideburns down to his chin, which is liberally sprinkled with stubble and the remains of scraped-off pimples, and is wearing a jacket with leather tassels, a dandruff-ridden comb in his breast pocket. The play of his facial muscles indicates a chewing gum in the area of his rear molars and his skin colour indicates jaundice, or a couple of unblocked punches to the liver region. But the one with the sideburns only looks in good condition at first glance. Bodybuilding and steroids in some fitness studio don't make a man a fighter. And the blond one? His strapping gait is so stiff that I'd guess at a slipped disc.

And there's nothing to say he knows how to use his weapons.

The sweat on the landlord's face has evaporated. He stands motionless behind the bar until the men come to a stop in front of him. The foam collapses in the glasses below the beer tap and a cup of hot chocolate clouds over with a trembling skin. The landlord takes his hands out of a sink, summoning the two men into the kitchen with a barely perceptible nod of his head and following them without drying his hands. From my table, all I can see through the gap in the door is parts of the blond man, sitting on a swing-lid garbage can with his legs apart, massaging his knuckle-dusters.

Then the door is torn open again and a child races in. The landlord's son—no doubt about it. The same dark curls, long nose and skin like white parchment. A happy-go-lucky five-year-old in a blue snowsuit, dragging a wet sledge behind him with a clatter. He's saying goodbye to a playmate on his way back to the park, while his mother is still outside talking to a neighbour, the florist. The little boy walks past my table, leaving a trail of black sludge. He pushes open the kitchen door. The sledge holds it open, enlarging the gap for a moment, and I can see how his father raises his arms in shock as his son runs toward him.

Then all I can see is the blond man's chubby fingers scooping up the child and setting him down on his lap. The boy struggles, slips off and runs to his father.

Sneakers with open tongues kick at the sledge, the door swings shut again and robs me of my view. I stare at the door, imagining the blond thug's hand reaching for the child's locks again, until the image becomes the end of a tunnel that I have to get out of as soon as possible.

I stand up.

It's only one pace to the bar, Mirca's tray still standing on it. I put the dirty glasses in the sink and stand still. As I breathe, pressing air into my lower abdomen, I watch beer dripping in white flakes from a leaky tap onto the drip tray, collapsing into sluggish trails of thin foam and slowly vanishing into the draining holes. What remains is a feeling of emptiness and concentration.

I take half a turn toward the kitchen. The door is melamine-coated. Granite-coloured plastic dotted with green and red sprinkles imitating the surface of rough stones. As I press my right hand against it, the draught presses a narrow strip of food scent into the cafe. My sense of smell registers it in several layers, breaking it down into vegetables, pastry, meat, spices, cleaning fluid. Now the tiles. They're on the side wall, to the left and right of a chrome extractor hood; pale grey, matte tiles woven through with a haze of dark grey.

The blond man is still perched on the bin. I can see his parting, an irregular jagged line of scalp leading to a ragged whorl of split ends just before his hair falls back onto the rear of his head; I can see his high forehead dotted with blackheads and his nose, a web of tiny red and blue veins at its tip a sign of alcoholism. Before the man can even form a facial expression in response to my appearance, I ram the tray into his neck. The wooden edge hits his Adam's apple. He utters a sound rather like the breaking of dry wood, collapsing over the trash can. I hadn't reckoned with so little resistance. Nor with how repulsive it would feel to employ force against an unresisting body.

His friend reacts more quickly than I'd thought. I register a glittering projectile at head level. I turn away. The blade drives deep into a ham hanging above a row of bains-marie full of dumplings and vegetables. I deal a crescent kick to the knife-thrower's throat. His torso falls onto a pile of unwashed Brussels sprouts between the juicer and the hob, but his hand is already reaching into his pocket. I give a quick kick with my rear leg, completing my turn by ramming my index finger into his solar plexus up to the knuckle.

Wheezing. I turn around and take a look at the unnatural shade on the blond one's face. He's lying on the floor, struggling for air.

I pull the knife out of the ham and hold it into the bain-marie. Then I bend over the blond man and open his windpipe, an inch-long incision just below his Adam's apple. I turn to the landlord, still clutching his son in his arms. Behind his ear is the silver ballpoint pen. I pull it out, unscrew it, remove the cartridge and the rear part, dip the front end in hot water, bend back over to the blond man and insert the point of the tube into the cut. Five seconds of fear he might die. Then at last a sucking and whistling, sucking and more whistling. He's breathing with the trembling of the tube that I've stuck into his throat.

Now I stare at my hands, turning them over. My feet too, with their balls spread out to kick and their horned outer edges pressing against the seams of my shoes, are alien to me. The landlord leaps over, grabs me by the shoulders and sits me down on a chair.

At this moment, the child starts to yell. He's been standing there all along, pale and with his lips pressed tight. Now he cries out, running away from his father and disappearing into the cafe with a sob.

The landlord keeps his cool. He looks me in the face and says nothing at all, a long, sad look from brown eyes hemmed in by thick lashes.

Then he lays a hand on my arm.

'Thank you. My name's Mirca.'

I pull myself away and look at him. What does this man want, why is he thanking me? The blond man is sucking and whistling, sucking and whistling; his partner groans, turning aside, coughing and vomiting on the tiled floor. The landlord gets up, goes over to the freezer, opens it, fetches a bottle of vodka, takes an empty cup, fills it to the brim and presses it into my hand.

Burning trails of vodka run down my oesophagus, spreading out as a warm spot in my stomach. The landlord picks the knife up off the floor, taking an apron and wiping off the grip and blade before he puts it back in the man's pocket. Then he opens a door leading out to the backyard, a dark area with two parking spaces, windowless walls and an open drive onto the street.

He grabs the blond man under his arms, pulling him cautiously out of the door and dragging him outside. The other man he takes by the shafts of his cowboy boots, red-brown high-heeled boots with brass tips and spirals of decorative embroidery.

Then he comes back in, going straight to the freezer. He fetches the bottle, fills my cup with vodka a second time and asks me if I want anything to eat.

Afterwards, I'm back in the front room of the cafe again. The newspaper is still in its place, the patrons still sitting at their tables as before. In front of me is a steaming plate piled high with pasta and salad.

The old woman has finished her soup. Awkwardly, she opens the snapper of her purse and extracts a pillbox. The breakfasters have taken out books, playing with their champagne flutes and stubbing their cigarettes out on mayonnaise-soaked lettuce leaves.

I eat slowly, chewing every bite.

Mirca steps over to my table from the bar. He wants to know if I like the food. I should come back tomorrow, he says, or the day after, whenever I like. He doesn't give me a bill.

Not that day, and not on any other.

7

'It's OK. Let me get it.'

The man lifts his backpack onto the tabletop and opens it a crack, rummaging up to his elbow in clothes. With a grip as if he were bringing a calf into the world, he pulls out a handful of blue and red notes. He grasps them like pieces of cloth with his whole hand rather than his fingertips, stuffing Mirca's change casually into his pockets as well.

The gloomy light of the street lamps shines down on Weinbergsweg. The snow has almost melted, revealing the past year's chewing gum wrappers and lost gloves. We walk alongside one another, our heads lowered, me in my canvas sneakers lined with old newspaper against the cold, him in worn-down calf-high trekking shoes, held together by strings knotted to the remains of torn laces.

A police van comes toward us, its siren off but at a sharp speed. The van swings onto the pavement, sliding doors opening, and a six-strong troop of men in green jumps out before our feet. By the way the man next to me forgets to take a breath and forces himself to walk slowly, I can tell he's scared. I link arms with him, pulling him into the driveway of a chain-store bakery. We shove past a delivery van and climb over a concrete mesh fence. A path of old-fashioned studded concrete plates leads us to a series of interlinked backyards. In the middle is a new playground, a structure of wood, steel and red ropes embedded in sand. Now, at twilight, there are teenagers sitting on the poles, in a semi-circle of glowing red dots.

Indecisive, we stop at a row of empty wooden benches. My eyes wander upward to the rooftops black under the darkening sky. You can see my building from here, and even a tiny section of the handkerchief-sized fenced-in backyard.

I can see a light shining, a weak yellow flicker on the top floor. Ignoring my companion, I run straight across the playground to the back entrance of Number Fifteen. I leap down the slanting stone hollows of an old basement staircase, past roughly hewn wooden cellar partitions stacked with fresh coal briquettes. Behind them, precisely beneath the two buildings, is a meeting place from before the Wall came down. The seats and mattresses furnishing the cellar room are rotten now, only the names of forgotten Western pop bands still luminous blue on the walls. There's a connecting door to which I found the key in the apartment below mine in 1992.

I unlock the door and enter the basement of Number Fourteen. I hasten along a puddle-strewn gangway, stumbling over pickling jars, chair legs, mouldy folding canoes and empty boxes, and reach the steps that lead me upward.

I stop on the staircase, hearing footsteps. Behind me, the man with the backpack storms through the connecting door, coming toward me along the gangway. His back is hunched. He's taken his baggage off his shoulders, holding it to his stomach with his interlocked hands. He steers past the stray objects by pulling his head in, dodging, finally throwing down his backpack by the canoes and dragging it along the floor behind him by its strap.

He reaches the staircase and throws his luggage up the steps, placing a hand rough from frost on my shoulder and pushing past me. His jacket, worn smooth, strokes against my face. It smells of tobacco and old material, a protruding feather scratching my cheek. Before I can say anything he's picked up his bag again and disappeared.

I follow him out into the yard. A thin cloud of smoke is drifting out of the half-opened upper windows of Dunkel's kitchen. As I enter the side wing, I bend down for the flashlight I keep on a hook by the side of the door. I grab at thin air; it's not there any more. Cursing, I feel my way ahead, over foot-sized holes and linoleum edges curled up into trip hazards.

The door to Dunkel's flat is wide open. A stench of fire drifts toward me. The man has dumped his backpack in the doorway. I find him in Dunkel's kitchen. He's trying in vain to extinguish a burning shelf, beating with tea towels at the smouldering wood. Now he's discovered a broom, taking it in his hand and sweeping crockery, tins and baskets to the floor, stamping out flames. He stands helplessly between black-stained objects, shrugging his shoulders as he looks at me.

I run back into the corridor to my front door. My hands trembling, I unlock it and fetch a hosepipe from my kitchen cupboard, something I use as a shower in the summer. The man comes to meet me. He has patches of soot on his face, jacket and hands. The two of us return to Dunkel's kitchen together, push the hose over her tap, turn it on, aim it at the shelves and spray.

The flames are soon extinguished. Only now, exhausted and wading up to my ankles in a wet grey mush of smouldering remains, do I feel the pain in my lungs, the cold of soaked clothes. The man takes my hand and we walk down a flights of stairs, open the window to the yard and lean out.

Sirens, a screech of brakes, doors slamming. I jump with shock, bending forward, listening and staring out into the dark. The sound mingles with screams, rising and dispersing again. The windows of the building opposite are dark; no one seems to have looked over to us and noticed the fire.

'Come on, we'll go to my place.'

The hesitant, rather unpractised-looking smile on the man's creased face seems to express agreement. In two leaps, he jumps up the stairs ahead of me, shouldering his backpack.

'What's your name, anyway?' he asks in a hoarse voice at the back of my neck as we enter the door.

'Hell.'

I tap the sign with my name by the door, not looking round.

I can't imagine a greater contrast than between Dunkel's apartment and mine. At least bearing in mind that the layouts are exactly the same, mirrored across the axis of the stairwell.

Before we enter I take off my shoes and gesture to the man to do the same. We walk down my hall, the hall with hemp flooring and whitewashed walls. The door shuts behind us, blocking out the ashes, the stench and the chaos of strange events that I don't understand.

The man walks to the end of the hall and into my room. I go into the kitchen, put the kettle on and spoon tea into one of the delicately patterned pale blue porcelain teapots going cheap in every Chinese shop, a special harvest of green tea from Yunnan that Wang gave me last year to say goodbye.

When I enter the room with a tray a little later I'm irritated. Everything looks the same as usual. Honey-coloured floorboards, stripped and waxed, a small set of shelves on the window wall and in the middle of the room two tatami mats made of rice straw, which I use for sleeping and sitting on.

And then there's a pile. A pile of jacket and backpack blocking the way to the window between the bed and the shelves. And my visitor standing next to it, leaning on the wall and about to light a cigarette.

He catches my eye immediately. With his thumb and forefinger, he shakes the lit match out, puts his tobacco away again and sits down. We drink in greedy drafts, warming our hands on the hot cups, pouring second helpings.

Once the teapot is half empty he reaches into his back pocket, fetches out bright green fragments melted into bubbled lumps and puts them down at my knees. I touch them. They're still warm from the fire.

'I found these by the stove. Do you know what they might be?'

'Coal lighters.'

He lets time pass, fidgeting, changing his position, then he holds his body straight, sitting there with his legs crossed, his elbows pressed against his kneecaps.

'Someone laid that fire.'

He leans back, waiting for my reaction. I try to make my face look unmoved. There might be other, far more harmless explanations for everything, for the firelighters, for the tangle of cables in Dunkel's room and even for her disappearance. I wonder why the man is so interested in the whole thing. Now he jumps up, pacing to and fro across the room.

'Have you seen anyone around here recently who's not from the building?'

'Sure—today.'

'I mean, apart from me.'

'No. But someone used my flashlight. When I came in before and wanted to take it off the hook it wasn't there.'

His eyes flash into slits—cold, hard, full of suspicion. Then he relaxes again, looking at me.

'Houses like this were built a hundred years ago. Look at the knobs on my windows. Much too good for swollen frames with the putty crumbling away.'

I point a finger in the vague direction of the old gems of horn and decorated brass fastened to my windows. He doesn't look.

'Sometimes the plaster falls down on your head. The pipes burst on a regular basis, sending the neighbours' sewage and dishwater creeping up into our sinks. On sunny winter days the heat stocks on the blocked chimneys and presses sulphurous gases into the room. Old people who forget to air their rooms die in their sleep.'

I pour out the last of the tea.

'The water pipes are lead. A boy who lived in my building as a child was poisoned that way, a gentle, chubby five-year-old boy. He was always playing in the yard on his own and drinking drips from a leaky water pump.'

The man holds his cup in both hands, sweeping his eyes across the edge of the tatami mats. As if he had to avoid my gaze.

'The gas pipes run along the kitchen walls. Most of them leak. The stoves don't have a safety valve. As soon as you touch the knobs gas comes out. All it takes is a cigarette…'

'. . . from the visitor with the flashlight . . .'

'. . . to start a fire accidentally. Not to mention cable fires caused by the old wiring.'

I realize that Dunkel never has visitors, but I don't mention it.

'And the lightshow with the timer switch? Have you got an explanation for that?'

'No.'

The man looks embarrassed. As if I'd said some-thing wrong, ignored some kind of rule; I've no idea what rule. He gets up, turns to and fro, sliding aimlessly across my floor on woollen socks worn thin at the heel, and I think: He wants to leave now.

I take a step toward the stove in the corner and pull on my thick working gloves. It's time to put more coal on the fire. I turn the hot handle that opens the stove door and push the grating behind it aside with a poker.

The morning's embers have collapsed into a dark red pile almost covered with brown hills of ash. I scrape the remains downward with the poker, open the lower door and shake the handle of the ash drawer to even out the sand-like mass. Then I place eight black bars on top of the embers and close the top door again. A dull roar and a saturated orange glow tell me I've managed to re-light the stove.

By the time I turn around the room is empty, with light falling out of the kitchen. I can hear the man turning on the tap and the soap plopping into the stainless steel sink I only recently stole from a building site. He comes back shortly later, his face clean and hands washed. He stands in the doorway like in the hall across the corridor this morning, and looks at me.

My initial impulse is to run away. Running away is not only legitimate, it's also the best means of all in hopeless situations. The last of the strategies. The one you use when all others fail.

Then I realize there's no escape route. Behind me, the stove is lashing up to maximum heat, banning the frost from my back and sending it out to my limbs as goosepimples. Every movement is a movement directly toward him. But I can't stay put so I take a step, slowly, not letting him out of my sight. Metre by metre, the distance between us vanishes, and with it the hope that he'll let me past him in the narrow hallway without anything happening.

At the moment of my final steps, an exaggerated perception of the unfamiliarity of his body sets in. The square chin, the fissures in the dry corners of his mouth, the dirt under the nails of his fingers, which have stopped drumming against the wood of the doorframe, the curve of his collarbone, half covered by the bleached collar of his sweatshirt, torn into tiny lacy edges. Just before the threshold to the hallway, I return to his eyes, looking into the green, into pale eyelashes and the slightly reddened flesh of his eyelids where they protrude.

Chronic conjunctivitis, I think. He puts a hand out for my hair, touches it with his lips, pulls me to him, running the tip of his tongue along my neck. A sound comes out of my throat, deep and unfamiliar.

8

Waking up is bad.

It's not an emergence from sleep, more like falling out of an anaesthetized-like state. It holds my limbs still numb and captured, while my eyelids are mobile again, no longer offering protection to my eyes and sending them into the complete extent of the catastrophe with a brief blink.

There's a stench of burning above the whole neighbourhood.

I'm lying under the open window, feeling it blow in at me at irregular intervals as the wind turns. It's a mixture of dust, burnt rubber, blossoming lilac bushes. After a few breaths I feel nauseous.

A sour taste drives saliva into my mouth. I swallow it down but it rises straight back up. Just as I'm about to abandon all resistance to my nausea, my body's indignation sinks deeper. Long before I can persuade my sphincter of preventative measures, my intestines begin getting rid of burdensome matter.

After a while I manage to get upright. I prop my elbows on the horsehair and look around.

I'm alone — that's my first thought.

No man, no dog, no backpacks, no plastic bags. I'm alone with empty beer bottles, a dented folding table and a gas cartridge like the kind you use to cook at campsites. Daylight makes the room look larger. In the rear part is a scaffold of piled chairs. A second door, wide open, leads outside. Weeds grow in the sand on its threshold.

Only now, delayed, does the flight instinct come.

I sit upright and rip my underwear. As soon as I'm on my feet I want to run to the door, feeling a panicked impulse to get out. There's a rough barking and the sound of dog's paws approaching. A pale collie face appears in the doorway, looking at me in amazement, not unfriendly, seconds later pricking up its ears at a high-pitched whistle and disappearing again.

Before I turn to the exit my eyes alight on something under the camping table. I take a step closer and bend down. A brown leather pouch, two pipes. Not hesitating for a moment, I pick them up, stuffing them in the pockets of my cotton dress and leaving the building. Outside, I stand on a hill of pale brown, granular emptiness in a strong wind, the sun not yet warming the day. The dune-like elevation on which the house stands is in the part of the enclosure where there's no exit. One side of the sandy hill falls off steeply, ending at a wall; the other crosses over to the roof of a swimming pool in the shape of a ship, stuck with murky skylights reminiscent of chewing gum bubbles. To get away from here I have to climb down in the opposite direction and fight my way across the terrain to one of the exits in the middle section.

'Görlitzer Bahnhof.' The tannoy voice announcing the station sounds surprisingly close. At the same elevation as me, a train has released its brakes and is moving slowly across the bridge. I turn around, climbing down a track lined with grey bushels of grass.

The clock on the church tower at Lausitzer Platz shows a quarter past five.

Randomly distributed outhouses and piles of bizarrely shaped building materials hem in the site, tipped-over posts once lighting the tracks and shattered frosted glass from an old-fashioned box divided into lit rectangles, announcing the direction of the trains with a flare of light.

It's the very overview you supposedly have from a hill that I mistrust. I can't make out a soul anywhere, yet still apprehension has settled on my chest. With no cover, I'm exposed to all eyes far and wide. Not seeing anyone, not even at a distance, shores up my fear of being watched.

I look down at myself. My bare feet are enclosed by the trampled straps of brown sandals. Scoured by grains of sand caught in the sweat between the skin of my soles and the surface of the sandals, the balls of my feet are stinging. I look at my square toenails, brittle at the outer edges, the smallest nails almost disappearing behind swollen toe flesh, then black hairs on white winter legs blending seamlessly into kneecaps sprinkled with childhood scars—seeing everything with a precision that I sense will never leave me.

Impossible to walk onto the street in this condition —an idea that rises into fear. A fear that I might not manage the decisive step outside once I get down there, might be torn to pieces as I cross from this emptiness to the confines of the city, as if caught between two poles repelling one another.

Not finding the courage to take that step, I collapse against the slope. My heels prise open holes, sinking in to the ankles. My lower arms scatter my stomach and legs with sideways swipes of sand. My hands hurl up big lumps that I catch with my face, a thrashing and wheeling of all my limbs until I'm covered over and over with sand in every nook and cranny.

I lie still like this, feeling a weak sense of anger at wasting my energies. A slanted section of street appears in the view over my left shoulder, trapped in the studded steel of the railway line and cut off just behind the middle by two advertising hoardings fastened to the wall and jutting out above it, and right in the middle moves a dot with two legs, hardly thumbnail-sized from here, as if spat out onto the asphalt.

It's him. He's coming back.

A shock that my senses can't check. And yet it makes me get up instantly and walk. After a short run I come across a path branching off at an angle, cutting a swathe into the dense bushes around the edges of the terrain. It leads downward in a sharp curve, taking me to a large pipe set in stone, the tunnel under the former railway embankment. I run through the cool hollow strewn with glass, crumpled tissues and drink packs, clamping off my nasal breathing as I used to as a child to avoid the pissy stench of corners like this.

On the street is a telephone box. I approach the yellow cabin with large paces, drag the door open and breathe the musty scent inside. I lean my head against the grey coin-box and watch the door swinging back first slowly, then closing with a jerk. Through the plexi-glass window smeared with pigeon droppings, I see the remains of smouldering garbage containers filled with white spirits, building timber and old tyres. On the opposite side of the road a man-sized hole gapes in the window of a liquor store, white splinters of smashed glass glinting on the pavement.

A man comes walking along the cycle path, a thin balding figure in a denim jacket and beige old men's sandals. He's clutching two cloth bags and looks in at me. Does he want to make a phone call? I leave the call box to be on the safe side but then notice him crossing the street. He puts his bags down between the shards, clambers awkwardly through the hole and scours the shelves of the looted store for juice bottles, taking all the time in the world.

Presumably anyone walking around at this time of day is either drunk or occupied with their own business. I can just walk along the road in peace to the end by the water. I can slip inconspicuously into my borough of Neukölln, untouched by current affairs. Along Harzer Strasse, torn in two by the Wall, I can cut through the neat 1920s' estate built for public servants to the pistachio-coloured corner house greyed by the poor air. I can insert my double-bit key, push it through and pull it out again in the well-polished entrance hall, feel safe again at last.

The Landwehr Canal splits in two. The border looms pale grey, barbed wire planted on a bulge of concrete, illuminated by an army of curved lamps extending like spoons at the shades. The border to the next borough is inconspicuous in contrast; not to be made out either by the buildings or by the pavements marked by various epochs of paving and patching.

I reach Lohmühlen Bridge.

It's always quiet here. Where the Wall creates dead ends, the traffic is in a strange proportion to the width of the streets. You can cross the bridge but you come to a stop at the sector sign. Next to it is a wooden viewing platform for tourists. Except that barely anyone ever stumbles across it.

Anyone who doesn't know the area turns around again, overlooking the narrow staircase hidden by bushes, planted sparsely enough to push a way through. It leads to the opposite side of the bank and the other borough. Sometimes you have to climb over rough sleepers here, preferring the place's seclusion to nearby benches.

I have to turn onto the next street, which leads away from the water, then straight on and on, from driveway to driveway, from bike stand to bike stand. Keeping on between the barely one square-metre patches of earth strewn with faeces that trees have to make do with in cities.

The things grow nevertheless; they grow everywhere. I know one near the closed-off Reichstag, by a bridge named after a general. You can see it when you pass under the bridge on a tourist boat. Between weed-green blocks of stone, it has pushed its way out of a crack, a knotty, crooked maple that never sees the sky but still survives, a tough creature. Living on—that has to be the step, with clenched teeth, with my shoulder aching from the dog-bite and sandals slapping along the grass verges of Kiehlufer, and then the next, and then the next after that. Growth is nothing but walking on, dividing time from stone to stone and from leaf to leaf.

9

His name is Markus. Markus März, like the month of March. I asked him in the dark and he whispered it in my ear, a warm stream of air, a consonance of consonants against my eardrum. In the mountain range of night-grey bedcovers, his arm juts out like that of a giant. His head with its short hair, periodically lightened and then darkened again by the lamps on next door's staircase, is turned away from me. Perhaps he's asleep.

Clinking of glass. Scraping of crates on wet ground, interrupted by calls in stage whispers. The traders running a late-night liquor store with its back to my building are closing up for the night; I can hear them through my hall window. It can't be too late if the two of them are still there. Ten o'clock at most.

März shifts. He looks over at me, sits up, pulls on a shirt and pants. Then he stands up and busies himself with his backpack. It seems to have a second bottom, because this time he opens it from below. Something is stuck. He tugs at a hook. Threadbare material rips, a pack of bank notes springs out onto the floor. März hisses a curse, puts a hand over his mouth, turns around. Through a slit between the sheet and the blanket, I can see him crouched between scattered bank notes. Helpless eyes migrate to and fro between me and the money.

Minutes have passed by the time he feels for the first note. His eyes are fixed on my contours beneath the covers. Concentrated and soundless, he collects the money back up in slow motion. Like someone who's stepped onto too thin ice and is hoping to withdraw. Thousands, five hundreds, two hundreds. The sweat of fear disperses around the room. I count along with him, coming to ninety thousand. März folds the backpack closed, lashing buckles tight. I turn my head, moving the covers and stroking strands of hair out of my face.

'I'm going out for something to eat.'

His voice sounds firm.

'There's a kebab place on the corner of Choriner Strasse. Bring me one too. With garlic sauce, no chilli.'

His footsteps fall away. I leap up, reaching for my pants and sweatshirt.

He's left his bag here.

It's a Swiss army backpack made of grey canvas, with brown leather straps and several large outer pockets. You can get them at army surplus stores, along with plastic survival sheets, decommissioned mess kits and the kind of pocket-knives they say you can use to build a raft in an emergency. His money compartment is a kind of false bottom, very inconspicuous, with a zip concealed by Velcro; except the seams weren't strong enough.

I start by opening the outside pockets. The left one is full of dented tins containing bicycle tyre patches, chain lubricant and an Allen key. On the right I find his toothbrush, shaving kit and several sheets of multivitamin tablets sealed in plastic. The third of the outer pockets is on the front, tightly packed and closed with a metal buckle. I bore my fingers into its sides and feel a rolled-up towel, seemingly containing something hard at its core. Perhaps a soap case.

As I go in deeper I come across some kind of felt cloth. Curious now, I decide to open the pocket after all. I push the strap through the metal ring, pull up the flap and fetch out the towel, holding it by one corner. It unrolls. Something heavy, metallic and shiny extricates itself from the cloth and falls onto my bed. Not a sponge bag, nor a soap case—a gun.

I bend over, touching it cautiously on the barrel. My fingers are instantly oily. There's a catch on both sides of the wood-encased grip. I jiggle at it, press it, pulling it upward with caution. A spring releases, a mechanism pops up. Twelve bullets glint in the indentations of an ammunition cartridge.

Nobody walks around with a gun and nearly a hundred thousand marks in their bag for no reason. And then the story about Dunkel, the strange river journey, her disappearance. Two stories that don't fit together in the slightest. Perhaps März has come into money. But why would he need a gun then? People like that have credit cards—they don't stuff their assets in among their dirty socks.

A slam. The front door downstairs; März is coming back. Fear spreads across my body. My fingertips go cold, my mouth dry. There's no point in putting the gun away; it would even be dangerous. He might find out later that I've seen it, but he wouldn't know when.

First floor, second floor, heavy footsteps. You have to tackle critical situations directly, Wang says; you have to drive them on to their potential climax. If I make sure there's enough distance between him and the gun on my bed, nothing can happen, despite all else. Where will I find the determination to face him, when we were so close just before, his deep furrows touching my face, almost disappearing for a short time. How am I to know if I have to fight him? And when? And where would I find the strength for a blow?

Third floor. My skin sends an army of erected hairs to the fore. A black fuzz, tense for defence, but so easy to penetrate. This skin is far too thin, too narrow the boundary from outside to in, too easy to destroy.

The door is leaned to. März pushes it open.

I'm standing against the side wall leading to the hall. He, I and the gun form an oblique triangle. Oblique enough for him to pass through it if he wants to pick it up.

März appears in the doorway. He seems unruffled, no tension about him. The handles of two flimsy plastic bags are digging into his palms. They're packed with triangular kebabs wrapped in aluminium foil, and several cans of Coke. He holds the bags up in front of my nose, looking at me.

As I just stand there and look back, saying nothing and doing nothing, his mistrust rises. Again, it starts with his eyes; it's as if they were changing their consistency. All at once they're smooth and cold, like glass marbles that the children roll across the dry paddling pool in the park across the road. At the same time, the blood withdraws from his skin; it grows grey within seconds, dry and full of notches. Without moving an inch, he has distanced himself from me entirely.

Now comes the slow turn of his head. His eyes, wandering across the room, latch onto the open backpack and the gun, where they freeze for a moment. Then März turns back to me, raising his arms and dropping the plastic bags on the floor.

Silence. Garlic sauce runs across the floor between our feet, branching out into rivulets and seeping into the gaps between the floorboards. I can hear evening sounds from the distance: car horns, the bang of a car door closing, a tram ringing its bell, granulated clip-clops of high heels on the cobbles.

'Looks like you've robbed a bank.'

He twitches; no sense of humour. He takes a hectic breath, the buttons of his lumberjack shirt straining across his sternum. Red patches on his neck dance with the swallowing motions of his Adam's apple, until März has summoned up enough of a voice to answer.

'Yes, last Friday.'

Not waiting to see how I react, he falls back on a cushion behind him, laying his hands over his face. To be on the safe side, I move over to the bed close to the gun, up to the bullet cartridge. I take it in my hand, test the distance and throw it overarm into the coal scuttle.

'Why do you do it?'

'What?' He throws his head up.

'Rob banks. Why do you do it?'

'It was my first.'

He says nothing else, just staring at me. Then his eyes slip past me to the aerials of the neighbouring roofs. He's fighting, I can see it in his face. I can see his loneliness in the beginning crow's feet at the corners of his eyes. And his doggedness, fixed on a goal far outside himself. Far outside the two of us in this room, where the evening is gradually growing quieter, the night blacker.

'I grew up in a small town. Bad Homburg. A stinking rich area. Completely different to here.'

His hands wander into his sleeves, the left one under the right edge, the right hand under the left sleeve; his fists clench, pull at the material, creeping up to his elbows and encapsulating them.

'. . . freshly painted houses and expensive shops. People eating breakfast on the patio. A pedestrian zone. A spa park with an English lawn. Traffic lights everywhere. And plenty of spa visitors in their over-fifties, strolling from medicinal spring to medicinal spring clutching plastic cups.'

'Where is it exactly, Bad Homburg?'

'North of Frankfurt. It's not a suburb, but it's close. Behind it comes the Taunus.'

'Taunus?'

'A mountain range. With the rich people's villas along the edge of the forest.'

Why is he telling me this? The pressure with which he's pressing his voice out of his larynx gives me the feeling something about these descriptions is important to him, but he's not getting to the crux. He looks past me, rocking his lower arms clasped around his elbows, looking out of the window and talking, telling me about double garages and infrared surveillance systems, bluewindowed limousines, tennis clubs and spa balls, and about children giving each other silver watches for their birthdays.

'And your father? Is he one of them?'

He jerks.

'I mean is your father another one of those rich bastards?'

März is confused. Impatiently, he tries to liberate his hands from his shirt sleeves, tearing off a button and scratching his head.

'Well . . . not my real father . . . I mean, I don't know exactly, but . . . my stepfather is, yes.'

Stubborn silence.

He pulls his lighter out of his pocket, looks at the flint wheel and slides it over the tip of his thumb. Then he pulls up the left sleeve of his jacket, tugs at a few hanging threads, holds the lighter underneath them in great concentration and burns each of the threads away with a small flame.

What animosity people from the provinces can develop toward the places they come from. That's hardly possible in a city. There are too many impressions, too much change and speed for anyone to direct the repulsion of an entire childhood against the place.

Some days I walk through the city where I was born like a stranger in town; I ended up in Friedrichstrasse station recently. I was looking for a suburban train to take me to Bornholmer Strasse, and I was incapable of reading a sign or finding the exit in the midst of all the torn up and patched together architecture, resulting from two mutually exclusive political systems. I was caught in a jungle of symbols and labels, all their meanings premature or outdated. They referred to parts of the building that no longer exist, like the obtrusively jagged and yet squashed-looking letters of the *Intershop* that used to sell Western products for hard currency. Or to parts that aren't there yet, like the sticker for a lift that led me to an open shaft blocked off by a makeshift barrier of red and white striped construction site tape. After a long misdirected search I left the station, ground down by incompatible types of tiling, floor surfaces and escalators.

März has put his lighter away again, now reaching inside his jacket. A brief moment of vigilance seizes hold of me. But it's just a photo that he pulls out of his inside pocket, a colour snapshot the size of the palm of his hand, coated with a dense web of creases, tinged red and fraying at the edges where it's been held. He passes me the picture without a word, waiting for my reaction.

The street is the first thing I can make out, cobbles and two pastel-coloured Trabant cars parked on the slant of a high curb. In the middle of the shot is a factory gate, in front of it people in working clothes, perhaps twenty of them. The posts of the entrance are yellow brick, and alongside the street run tram tracks rather than a pavement. They lead into the factory yard. In the yard are wagons and man-high wooden structures that look like huge cotton reels. The factory building looms in the background, several storeys high and sombre.

I throw März a questioning look.

'Look at the people.'

I hold the picture up close to my face. Mainly men. Fairly young men, just a handful of women, all of them with short hair. Above one of the men's heads floats a thick cross pressed into the scratched gloss with a ball-point pen.

'Is that him . . . ?'

'Yes.'

'Your real . . . ?'

'Exactly. That's the factory where he used to work. Somewhere in East Berlin. No idea where. If he still lives here. If he's still alive at all.'

'Where you born here?'

'Yes.'

He hesitates. As if he were revealing something secret by answering.

'In Königs Wusterhausen, just outside Berlin.'

'How long did you live here?'

'Till I was three. But I can't remember anything. Unfortunately.'

'And your mother?'

'Took me to the West. My father was supposed to come after us but then he changed his mind. Or that's what she told me anyway. Not long after that she met my old man . . .'

'. . . Your stepfather.'

'Yes. From then on my real father never had a chance.'

He makes a sweeping who-cares gesture, reaches forward, takes a Coke can and plucks at the opening until it fizzes. Brownish foam shoots up at the edge of the lid, dripping over his fingers. He shakes it off, drops the tin ring and dries the back of his hand on the bed sheet.

'And what about you?'

'What?'

'Your parents, I mean.'

'Both dead.'

'Ah.'

He says nothing else but he watches me, his head askew.

'So you don't like your stepfather then?'

'Nasty piece of work.'

He rolls his pupils, frowning.

'He's a banker. On the board. A Very Important Man.'

'Is that why you rob banks?'

He shrugs.

10

I take the bus to the police station.

Stopping directly outside my front door, it loads up a group of sixty- to eighty-year-olds at ten-minute intervals and takes them to Karl-Marx-Strasse, where they eat cake standing up in draughty cafes or stream into the department stores to the hosiery, glove and hat departments. Bus journeys along the route are a carousel-ride of invalids. Anyone who can walk or has a bike avoids them. Most people go by car anyway. Nobody with money for taxis lives in this part of town.

I pull my key out of the lock, click one of its double bits into the hook on my keyring, push the metal ring over my middle and forefinger and hide my hand in the pocket of my cardigan, my fingers closed tight over the keys. Two paces take me across the pavement to the bus stop.

Even as the over-long bus rendered supple by a harmonica in the middle turns onto the street, still three blocks away, a jerk goes through the waiting crowd. Women open the fastenings of their purses held like breastwork fortifications, fetching out tickets. Impatient eyes rest on watches with penny-sized faces. Invalids tug crumpled document casings from the linings of overly tight breast pockets. Long before the bus pulls into the lay-by with its yellow and green post, almost everyone is clutching some kind of ticket entitling them to board, their arms outstretched: multiple journey tickets, single journey tickets and yellow senior citizens' stickers stamped zero-five for the month of May.

The man behind the wheel scratches the belly of his royal blue uniform. He inserts a cigarette between his teeth, whips out his platinum-coloured lighter and takes a nervous look in the rear-view mirror. His thumb sways impatiently above the button on the dashboard that folds the doors together again. He'd love to shut half of the passengers out, just leave them waiting for the next bus out there; you can tell by looking at him.

With the aid of trembling elbows and walking sticks peppered with medallions, each passenger seeks out a seat. I insert myself into the standing space equipped with hanging straps opposite the exit, squashed in between a tarpaulin shopping trolley and a stroller containing a two-year-old chewing on the teat of a bottle of tea, his face smeared with strawberry ice cream.

We cross the bridge over the canal. A sharp brake manoeuvre sweeps a folding rain bonnet belonging to a woman with violet-rinsed hair along the aisle. I turn around to pick it up but the child gets there first. He reaches for the plastic bonnet, running his fingers along the folds. Then he discovers his find is transparent. Delighted, he holds the plastic up to his eyes; but then his mother's hand intervenes.

We are spat out at Hermannplatz. The old people wander over the crossing to the bus stop in the other direction, screeching platitudes at one another that are torn away by the noise of the evening rush-hour. Scissoring sideways, I escape the former passengers and make my way to the curb of an island in the middle of the road, the pedestrian lights switching to green.

I can't think of anywhere less deserving of the name *square* than this Hermannplatz, an intersection dotted with confusing traffic lights from which the dual carriageways of the southeast emerge in a star-shape. Two stretched-out blocks of department stores and chain-store boutiques frame it. Between them, rather like an island in the traffic, is a rectangular terrain paved with small stones, on which a poorly stocked market camps out on four out of seven days.

I'm soon wedged between the stalls, sucked into the typical potpourri of useless and ugly things constituting the local spending sprees: vermilion polyester leggings and poorly sewn purses embroidered with plastic beads,

hung between large-patterned bales of cloth like washing on a line, sneakers with tiny lights embedded in their
heels that flash as you walk, raffia tapestries printed
with signs of the zodiac, phosphor headbands and
braces connected by a leather strap at chest level, the
size of a cigarette packet and fastened with a press stud.

On the margins of the white barrier to the street,
men gather in twos and threes on the few benches next
to overflowing garbage cans smeared with mustard and
old chewing gum, hoping to chat up girls, make dodgy
deals or pretend to someone that they are. No one else
stops here. Most people hurry past, loaded with large
shopping bags containing quilted covers, video
recorders, toys and huge amounts of fruit and vegetables.

The train tunnel below my feet issues a warm eddy
of air. I stand on a rhombus-shaped grating over the tunnel, pressing the palms of my hands to the densely
woven material tightly enclosing my legs. A deep-seated
reflex linked to the expectation that wind from below
will hurl the material upwards; but it's related to phan-
tom circumstances—I haven't worn a skirt for weeks
now. I leap off the grating, making my way to the other
side of the street.

After ten minutes' walk I arrive at the police station,
a fume-blackened Prussian public building. Between an
industrial yard and a petrol station, it closes the line of
buildings in the block, with plinths and window arches
of hunchbacked stones and window bars on the lower

floors that must be from the original period. In two paces, I cross the small hall behind the entrance door, my crepe soles squeaking up dove-grey stairs laid with airport PVC.

The reception is a through-room painted yellow. A counter, tattered at the edges into pressboard layers, cuts it into two narrow strips of corridor. On the wall next to the clock, two men suffering from the effects of insomnia gaze down reluctantly from a Wanted poster. Below them is a steel beam with a couple of bowl-shaped seats screwed onto it.

As I enter the room I discover the duty officer's cushion-like back. He's sitting at one of two desks pushed together lengthways, filling out a form with one hand while the other grasps the handle of his coffee cup.

I walk up to the barrier. The policeman drops his pen and turns around. A tall, very overweight man, not much older than me. He gets up with some difficulty, moving toward the counter and looking at me.

I describe what I'm here for in two sentences.

The man seems to shrink as I talk. His shoulders droop, he leans forward slightly and his jaw drops. Even before my voice has fallen silent, he has removed his watery grey eyes from our sightline and fixed them upon the rubber writing mat on the counter between us, a pen attached to it on a metal chain.

Then he goes back to his desk, picks up the telephone, jabs cautiously at the buttons with his fat forefinger and waits. After a while he hangs up and dials again, listening at the handset in reluctant tension. He only gives up after the third attempt, sighing and opening up a flap in the counter, and steps over to my side.

'Come with me.'

I follow him through a semi-glazed swinging door into the corridor behind, past waste bins with top-mounted ashtrays, a drinks vending machine and posters giving tips for preventing burglaries.

The officer leads me into a windowless room with ventilation slits in the ceiling. It is furnished with a number of scratched wire chairs chained together at the legs and a table scattered with leaflets.

'You can take a seat here. It'll be a while yet.'

The policeman leaves the room. I start to wait. As I wait I get cold. I've been having freezing attacks for days; it comes over me out of the blue and often stays for hours while the heat rises outside, the hottest spring for years.

The door is torn open with gusto.

Two uniformed officers enter, shoving a child into the room—an Asiatic-looking girl in dungarees and canvas sneakers. She's wearing a door key on a leather string around her neck, on her back hangs a satchel like a sandwich-shaped hump.

'You can wait here, OK?'

'We're going to get your mum and bring her here.'

The men are still talking but they're already turning on their heels. Their high tone of false friendliness, pitched too loud for the room, is that which adults like to use on children to keep them at a distance.

Then we're alone.

The girl sits down. She puts her school bag on the vacant chair next to me, a felt-pen-stained plinth over which she peers at me. She shuffles her legs forward until the backs of her knees are hanging over the edge of the seat, lowering her head and swinging her feet. Steps sound out in the corridor and move away again. Above our heads, a neon tube with a loose contact flickers.

11

'You've got to put the money in a locker.'

März squirms. He tips to one side off his cushion, kneeling and pulling himself to his feet, and starts to pace across the room. Three half-length paces from the bed to the door, five from the door to the stove, a stiff about-turn, no eyes for the coal scuttle, then five paces back to the hall.

I tear open the foil package. The kebab is cold now, a flapping muzzle of bread saturated with fat, stuffed with scrapings of veal and strands of purple pickled cabbage. I bite into it listlessly, twice, three times until my hunger subsides, then I take the second can of Coke to wash it down. As I try to prise it open, the tin ring-pull refuses with a slight crack, breaking off. A hundred and fifty yards of pacing—only then does März venture his first look at me, toward the window. Not changing my position, I reach into the shelves behind me. On the top shelf is a dish of stones. I feel for a round, cherry-sized one.

Three more laps pass before März realizes it's too late to undo anything; I'm just as tangled up in his story as he is in mine. With the pressure of the ball of my hand, the stone presses the stamped tin of the can opening into my Coke. He stops with a jerk, bumping his nose on the protruding round tile used to seal the stove's ventilation system. He stares into the coal scuttle, raising one hand and letting it fall again. Then he turns around, makes a leap onto the bed, throws the gun minus its magazine into his backpack, empties the outside pockets, stuffs a bundle of banknotes into his trousers, fastens belts, Velcro and buckles and whispers:

'Let's go.'

A net curtain of capricious snowflakes veils the abandoned Rosenthaler Platz. The buildings on the acute corners that meet at the square loom ahead of one another: sex shop, bookstore, pet shop, like one bow to another in a circle of moored ships. März has pulled a black knitted hat low over his brow. He walks very slowly. The open tips of his down jacket swing to and fro, the cold metal of his zip brushing the back of my hand. He takes my arm but our ways of walking aren't at all compatible. My attempt to adapt my small steps to the reach of his long legs only creates unpleasant syncopation. At the entrance to the underground station I tear myself free and take three steps down at once, but he catches me up, shaking his head.

And so we walk on. Passing the narrow Linienstrasse dotted with building sites at its corners, over wet wooden boards pressed into the torn-up cobbles, past barriers and the yellow twitching of warning lamps. Under dripping scaffolding, where the shops beckon with reductions announced in green and orange, along the closely embracing house fronts in the narrow alleys of Sophienstrasse and Gipsstrasse, their decay rendering them far more vulnerable with their spindly shapes than the stout Prussian blocks on the wider streets.

At the suburban railway bridge, I head for the staircase. Zoo or the Central Station in the East or Lichtenberg; every train from here will take us to the left luggage areas at the mainline stations, but März refuses a second time. He stops walking and leans against a locked-up snack van, rolling a cigarette, lighting it and blowing the smoke in my face in a greasy cloud thickened by his steamy breath. Then he turns on his heel and trudges underneath the railway bridge, not even looking to see if I'm following him. As if he'd had this locker plan all along and had just been waiting for me to prompt him. He wants to choose the route himself, of course — unnecessary obstinacy, at the wrong time and on the wrong issues.

März picks up speed, leaving me behind and marching toward Alexanderplatz. At the Red Town Hall a lone car turns onto Spandauer Strasse, a yellow and black light on its roof. I take a step onto the cycle path, gesture at the driver and shout through the thickening snowflakes:

'März!'

He turns around.

'März, we're being stupid! What have you got all that money for? Come on, let's take a taxi!'

Berlin Central Station is a squat building in the East, equipped with a complicated system of driveways and access routes. The cool smoothness of the floor, made of stone rather like black pudding, sprinkled with brown flecks and polished matte, provides the perfect camouflage for vomit and pools of beer. The usual suspects are holding out by the doors over the winter. They've entrenched themselves behind sacks of multiple wrinkled plastic bags pushed inside one another, which they are constantly rummaging in, exhausted by their futile battles against the security companies that send in freshly shaven troops every eight hours. The display case for the departure times is mounted in the belly of a brightly coloured larger-than-life plastic silhouette wearing a hat and clutching a suitcase, its steel feet anchored to the floor. Next to it, an open staircase leads to a kind of shopping gallery, emanating the fug of station consumerism though its signs are switched off for the night.

The station bar is still open. A man's back is visible through the window; he's leaning forward as he sits at the counter. He raises his glass, drains it and climbs down from his barstool. His keyring, fastened to his belt loop on one side with a snaplink, slips out of his pocket and dangles at hip level. He grabs it, sticking it back into his front pocket and stuffing the corner of his wrinkled shirt into his jeans.

März has found a board with pictograms and points at the suitcase with a key suspended above its handle. We walk back to the rear of the hall. A niche is fitted out from floor to ceiling with scraped and scratched lockers. We stop at an opening at waist level. März takes his luggage from his back, gropes a two-mark coin out of his chest pocket and inserts it into the slot.

The locker is narrow and goes back a long way. He lifts his backpack, heaving it up to the opening to shove it in.

'Shit.'

The backpack is jammed.

März clenches his teeth, still pushing, pressing his shoulder against the backpack—in vain. Now he's getting angry. He tugs at the stiff backbone with its leather shoulder straps, gets entangled in the loops, waves his arms to free himself, manages it but tears the skin of his lower arm on the protruding prong of a buckle.

'Stop it. You won't get it out otherwise.'

März breathes out through his nose with a snort, throwing me a shut-up look and kicking the lockers, twice. Then he fumbles with the backpack again, bracing himself and pulling until it falls toward his chest. From behind it flutters a loose leaf of a newspaper, BRITISH INVESTOR BUYS OBERSPREE CABLE FACTORY.

Distracted, my eyes pick out blue-black headlines framed by advertising, above two photos of an industrial complex. One shows a dock for barges, the other the front of the buildings, with workers driving into the yard from the street in open goods wagons. It's not until the last moment, just before my eyes go to turn back to März, that I discover the reels. Huge wooden discs, joined into pairs by an axis, roll from perception to recollection, looking for a point of contact, some kind of hollow where they might get caught and come to rest. And then I know, I know what the things are used for, what März's father must have used them for as well: cable drums.

From the other side of the hall a pair of guards approaches, trained to react to sounds of vandalism. Hurried, soundless rubber-soled footsteps, hands on their walkie-talkies and an even gait learned at anti-stress courses. I tap März on the shoulder, pointing toward the uniformed men and making the flat-handed gesture used to subdue aroused emotions: don't panic.

So we stay where we are and wait, März diagonally behind me with his pack at his feet, me standing up straight with my ankles shoulder-width apart, knees barely perceptibly bent and pointing slightly inwards. At the entrance to our niche they slow down, a fidgety pale blond man with tinted pilot's glasses and his once impressive older partner, radiating diffuse mental instability—a typical former East German police officer. Two pairs of eyes check the wall of lockers, then us. The bespectacled one glances at his metal-linked digital watch, his partner scratching the groin of his dull grey trousers. The two of them apparently aren't yet sure whether to speak to us.

A clatter of kicked-over bottles. An uncontrolled throaty shout rings out from near the staircase. The last guest has left the bar and is losing grip of his motor skills. He sways, trying to hold onto something, grasps at thin air and collapses on the floor plate of a downward escalator. The security guards react instantly to the new sound. Still facing us, they are already refocusing their attention in the other direction, rotating their heads in short alternating quarter-turns. I let out a breath of relief.

A quiet clicking. März has stood up, a down-blue, brandishing shadow at the corner of my eye. Then I hear his voice, scraping and high, almost breaking:

'Stay where you are. Don't take another step.'

The men's faces change colour, an unhealthy green shadow spreading across the older one's cheeks from his nostrils while the line of the pale man's chin breaks out in flecks of allergic red from his neck to his ears. I take a step back and try in vain to make eye contact with März. He's stepping from one foot to another, awkwardly shouldering his luggage, a dithery dance of all his limbs around his stiff-stretched right arm, the extension of his idiotic gun, its barrel pointing irretrievably forward and leaving me no other option but to make myself his accomplice.

'Give us your walkie-talkies. And stand back to back.'

I gesture at the floor and destroy the radios falling at my feet from limp hands with a stamp on the buttons as my mind turns in circles, cursing März. Perhaps I should have sent him back to Allee der Kosmonauten, told him to stare at the walls in his apartment or book a flight overseas.

The two men are leaning against each other now. The younger one pees in his uniform, the older man is trembling. I position my hands slightly splayed at hip level, take a breath and fold them apart like a locust, as Wang taught me. I smile a reassuring smile, pressing my thumbs and forefingers to their carotid arteries. März watches them collapse, his eyes wide. Then he puts his gun away and runs.

I clench my fists and press my lips together as we make it to the nearest staircase, which leads to a weakly lit tunnel with exits to the platforms. Before the first two exits, I manage to grab März by the sleeve. I point at the symbol for the local trains and drag him toward the platform.

The escalator gives a brief stutter and shudders into motion, carrying us up to the hammering sound of a pre-war train and the bitter scent of its brake pads, while a resigned female voice announces the departure of the last westbound train. Just before we reach the top, the warning signal rings out prior to the doors closing. März sprints to the rear door of the last car, pushes two slammed doors back open and leaps on. I run after him, he pulls me into the compartment and we move off toward Jannowitzbrücke station, accompanied by the sharp curses of the platform manager amplified across the tracks.

The train interior is strewn with a dense forest of illegibly intertwined characters with multiple upstrokes, all across the windows, seats and walls. März throws himself across a pair of seats, shoves his backpack underneath his head and breathes, his neck contorted by his luggage, his rib cage rising and falling violently. He coughs and clears his lungs, sits up and coughs again, opening the top window and spitting a clump of mucus into the night, splayed onto the window behind us by the wind and clutching on like a yellowish green beast.

By the time März turns back I'm standing in front of him.

He presses himself up off the seat with the balls of his hands, craning his exhausted face toward me. I reach out an open hand for him and touch the metal tag dangling just below his neck.

März makes no resistance, no motion.

Slowly, I pull the zip downwards, feel for the gun in the inside pockets of his jacket and pull it out. Then I raise my arm, aim at the open window and sling the weapon out into the darkness.

März swallows.

As the gun races toward the surface of the water like a black wingless bird, the train winds along the river Spree with a sluggish screech, almost at the station now.

12

Whoever brought this child up has taught her not to
expect any help from strangers.

She gets up, opens the flap of her schoolbag sport-
ing orange cat's eyes, pulls out a lunchbox from between
exercise books and a sports kit, and starts eating a
Danish pastry in mouse-sized bites, still taking no notice
of me. After a while the girl puts her food aside, fetches
out a cloth-covered screw-top flask, opens the lid and
puts it to her lips. Two dark red drops fall into her
opened mouth.

She puts the flask back into her bag, not looking at
it. The girl's eyes are fixed firmly on the ventilation slits
on the opposite wall. She concentrates on the movements of her hands, as if she could take back the entire
procedure by carrying out each action exactly in
reverse, lowering the flask, screwing closed the lid
fastened to its neck by a plastic cord, stowing the flask
in the empty space between books and sports kit.

'Shall I get you something to drink? There's a machine in the corridor.'

The girl looks over at me briefly but makes no reply. Perhaps she doesn't understand me. I repeat my question, forming my hand into a cup and raising it to my mouth. The child remains silent.

I stand up, go to the door, open it and look out into the corridor. A vending machine is mounted on the wall to my right. I insert a fifty-pfennig piece in the slot and press the button for hot chocolate. A cup springs out of the shaft, followed by a watery liquid that grows gradually darker, finishing with oily drips.

The girl has stood up on my return to the room, hot drink in hand. She hesitates toward me and then stands in front of me, reaching her arm out with her lips already half open. She takes the cup from me, holds her face over it and wiggles her nostrils in disgust, handing me back the hot chocolate.

'I'm Chinese.'

Astounded, I reach for the cup with a rather too sudden movement. Liquid spills over the back of my hand and into my cardigan sleeve, running down my arm to the elbow and meeting up with a rivulet of sweat descending from my armpit with no sense of heat, a web of wetting coolness.

'Only babies drink milk in China; it makes grown-ups ill.'

The girl gives me a provocative look, reaching behind her neck for her plait and fingering at a pink-varnished hair-slide decorated with tiny ladybirds.

'There isn't any milk in it. They only have water-based hot chocolate in machines.'

She hesitates, looking at me with distrust. Then she takes the cup, raises it to her mouth, drains it without a pause, crumples it and throws it in the waste bin under the table.

We sit down and wait again.

Time trickles by like molasses. The heater behind my legs is regulated by a central control system that hasn't yet reacted to spring, and radiates stuffy air. Whereas cold caused by real outside temperatures doesn't bother me any longer, this heat that doesn't make me warm wears me down all the more. Cold has been seeping into my innards from an unidentifiable place for days. All I can do is sit and wait for it to pass, moving as little as possible so as not to enlarge the tear.

'Do you want to play a game?'

'Depends.'

'Battleships. I'll draw the grids.'

The girl pulls an exercise book with a cover of green plastic out of her bag. With careful and deft movements, she removes a squared double page, folds it sharply in both directions and tears it into two equal halves. She holds the sheets of paper out to me. I nod. She takes a textbook, lays it across her lap, pulls a fountain pen out of a loop in her pencil case and begins to draw lines, lettering them. She makes two mistakes with the numbers, reacting with impatient sighs and looking for an ink eraser. Meticulously, she deletes the wrong markings, writing over the rough patches with a correction pen.

Then the girl hands me a pen and paper.

'Five twos, five threes, three fours, three fives and one six.'

Silence as we mark out our squares.

Then she raises her head, tossing coordinates in my direction. Two hits; my turn. I make an unsuccessful attempt, losing my first ship in the second round.

'Why are you here anyway?'

She screws the cap onto her fountain pen, lowers the paper and folds her hands across the grid.

'We have to go back to China.'

'You and your family?'

'Me and my mother. My father's staying here.'

'Why should your father stay and not you?'

'He's a student here. He's got a scholarship.'

'And where's your mother now?'

'Probably at home. They picked me up from school.'

The girl has turned away, pressing her lips together and concentrating on her table. The next few minutes pass with the crossing off of small squares. She greets two clumsy attempts to let her win with disdainful tuts. Not much later, I've beaten her.

Unperturbed, the girl throws her paper away, takes out a reading book and immerses herself in a page illustrated around the edges with street corners and traffic signs. I stretch, placing my cold fingertips on my temples, and wonder whether I ought to go back to reception, to ask the fat man if he's forgotten me.

A hand touches the door handle from outside.

It presses it down and the mechanism clicks. The door opens a hesitant chink and a female enters the room, a woman in flat canvas shoes and a strawberry-red raincoat. She's tied her blue-black hair back with a rubber band. She has high cheekbones and restlessly blinking eyes behind aluminium-coloured glasses frames that cover half her face.

A smile darts across the girl's face. She stands up and walks over to the woman. The woman looks at me, stretching her arms out. But they don't pull the child into an embrace; they take her by both hands as she squats down with a straight back until her eyes are on the same level as her daughter's.

They start a conversation I don't understand.

Not only the words are alien to me; their sound is too — a chain of semi-length syllables strung along a cord of tones that I can't follow. The unvoiced initial sounds are sharpened to a point, the vowels laid uniformly in their consonant bed, and there's no melody that might reveal what's a question, an exclamation, an answer.

The woman seems to be telling her daughter some-thing. She listens and nods, making brief interjections. Then the girl starts telling her something. Her mother leans her head to one side. Her features don't betray any emotions. Once or twice, the two of them look over at me. I try to put on a friendly smile but it feels like a gri-mace; I'm getting colder again.

In the end the woman gets back up, just as quickly and smoothly as she squatted down. She turns, the ends of her skirt and coat whirling against her ankles, and sits down on the chair next to mine.

For a brief, warm moment of pressure her hand closes around my fingers. She tells me her name. Wang. Then comes a sentence familiar from language-learning books.

'I'm very pleased to meet you.'

Her unvoiced sounds are hard, almost spat, and those tones are back again, singing high, swinging and descending again steeply, only that they have no place in our language, swaying directionless across the words' constituents.

The woman takes a purse out of her coat pocket to give me the money for the hot chocolate. I raise my hands in a gesture of refusal. My cardigan sleeves slip down, revealing the frosty skin tense around my arms. Surprised, her eyes dart along them, wandering across my face, testing, devoid of sympathy but not unfriendly. She adjusts her glasses and for a moment the tension in her face gives way to a friendly twitch at the corners of her mouth.

The door opens again, letting in a section of conversation underlain with corridor sounds, which is quickly ended on entering the room.

The two uniformed officers are back.

They are both young men with brown hair. One of them has a moustache, the other has short hair with startlingly long sideburns and a wedding ring. Not looking at the girl, they approach Wang. Her daughter has sat down next to her, her schoolbag jammed onto her lap. Their backs straight as poles, eyes open wide and their hands on their knees, the two of them wait to see what's going to happen to them.

The man with the short hair holds his hand out to Wang.

'Hello, Frau . . . Ying.'

Wang gives a brief uncomprehending nod. The girl stands up as if someone had called her to attention.

'Wang! Our name's Wang. In China the first name is always the surname.'

Wang puts a hand on her daughter's arm. She sits down again. The short-haired officer turns around to his colleague. It's only now that I notice how sheepish he looks. A semi-whispered exchange, then the second man steps forward, this time turning to the girl.

He clears his throat, his arms dangling.

'Can you translate for your mother? Tell her we're sorry. We made a mistake. Got the names muddled up. You can go home now.'

Turned to face her mother, the girl says two sentences. The tension vanishes from the woman's back. She blushes, bending forward and rubbing the toes of her canvas shoes together. The man with the wedding ring looks at her uncertainly, seemingly waiting for something, but she doesn't notice. She picks up her bag, takes out a container, opens the lid and passes it to me. It's full of closely packed filled pastries. I hesitate.

Three short, hissed syllables.

'You don't have to be polite,' her daughter translates.

I take a pastry and put it in my mouth. I must have been hungry since this morning. Now she holds the container out to the policemen. The unmarried one goes red, his colleague shuffles his feet.

'No thanks,' they call almost simultaneously, then turn around and leave the room.

A giggle slips out of Wang's throat. She points her index finger at the embarrassed men's shoulders as they close the door behind them. Then she takes a breath and gives me a laboured explanation, smuggled with some effort through the gates of her heavy accent:

'Luck is when someone else's kite string breaks.'

13

We've sobered up.

Two in the morning, the snow's melted and Rosenthaler Platz is a water-slicked abandoned intersection with no centre. März hasn't spoken since the incident at the station, trotting along at my side like a wet, maltreated dog. I've buried my hands in the pockets of my anorak. They feel feverish and feeble and the pressure upon two throats, left and right of the Adam's apples, is still adhering to the tips of my thumbs and forefingers. The lights on the corner of Lehniner Strasse have gone out, three street lamps broken by thrown stones. We feel our way into the building, stepping in a puddle. There's a smell of urine impregnated with hops and März, who seems to have a hole in his shoe, lifts his leg with a harsh whining tone.

He takes his shoes and socks off outside my front door and vanishes into the kitchen with a surly look to wash his feet. It's cold in my room—we left the window open. The stove has gone out and objects from März's backpack are scattered across the crumpled covers of my sleeping mats: tools, the soap case, a little notebook, a map of Berlin.

I take the map and flap it open. One of those patent-folded ones, the most common brand in Berlin. I sit down on the bed and flap my way southeast, fold by fold. Oberspree Cable Factory, it must be on the river somewhere. Outside the suburban circle line the industrial areas set in, outstretched pink-tinged buildings on a pale yellow background. Directly next to a bridge, I find what I've been looking for. The thin, slanting letters *KWO—Kabelwerke Oberspree*—are suspended above a building complex close to the water. The river Spree divides the neighbourhood into two halves, Ober-schöneweide and Niederschöneweide, and März doesn't seem to realize he was very nearly there.

He comes back barefoot, leaving a wet trail behind him and reaching for a towel from my shelves. He puts it on the floor in front of him, tramples his feet on it, undresses and then comes over to me. Not seeking my eyes, he sits down next to me, pulls up a cover, wraps himself in it up to his chin and lies down with his head on my pillow. He stares straight up, to where damp has been in the process of loosening the plaster over several years. Melding with the paint, it has formed variously convex structures, some of which, held only loosely by cobwebs, are suspended just below the ceiling. Not moving his head but turning his eyes in my direction, März whispers:

'Those guys aren't dead, are they?'

Irritated, I shake my head, stamp over to the door, switch off the light, lie down next to him and push his hand away as he tries to touch my forehead. März turns away, pulls the cover over his shoulders and has fallen asleep minutes later.

I lie awake, my eyes wandering across the dark contours of the room. I don't fall asleep until the early hours of the morning, as the first tram rumbles over the points on Zionskirchplatz. Now the map is unfolded entirely, right out to the little-used uncrumpled outer edges. Karow and Waidmannslust are settlements hugging green spaces, buttoned into slanting triangles and shapes, a loose web laid across the thin trace of the grid by the yellow ropes of the main roads. Shining lime green, the forest areas are dissected by paths, covered in a pattern of omega-shaped tree symbols, and in the West hangs a heavy, knotting and re-splitting braid of motorway.

I'm in the centre, somewhere between N12 and T7, and this centre is gradually disintegrating. Crumbs of former green are stuck to the Tiergarten, shabby with use. The Victory Column and the Brandenburg Gate have disappeared entirely into the creases.

But the worst is the area around the north of Neukölln—all that's there is a hole.

I know I'm slipping toward the hole, about to enlarge it with a rip caused by my weight at any moment, only to tumble into the darkness behind it. My attempt to shift my centre of gravity by leaning my head to the northwest is rather ridiculous, but it works. Slowly, I slide on my belly, my neck angled as far as possible in the direction of my flight, across the grazed glossy paper toward Moritzplatz. Across the remains of housing blocks, fire stations, church crosses and car park symbols, past taxi ranks, blue-framed public toilets, the double wave symbol of the swimming pools and the bus route lines thickened like knots at the stops.

On Fraenkelufer, a tip of my clothing catches on the comb-like hachures of a postcode boundary. I manage to tear myself free with momentum and roll to the canal, where I come to a stop lying exhausted on the grass of a park marked with dotted symbols. I look back to see a rip advancing toward me, following my route and almost upon me. All that's ahead of me is the water. In the water, I think, I'll be lighter. The tear can't get to me then. Head over heels, my knees pushed straight, I dive into a blue that doesn't feel wet, a print layer the colour of sky on a beautiful day that carries me eastwards.

By the time I open my eyes again it's early afternoon. The first ray of direct sunshine is falling into the room from the yard, a weak yellow square next to the stovepipe, spotted with pale flecks through the window's contorted refraction.

März is snoring.

I push the cover off carefully, pull on another sweater over yesterday's clothes, reach for my anorak and creep out to the hall. I put on my shoes in the corridor. The sharp stench of fire from yesterday has given way to a faint, indeterminate smell of burnt matter, as it settles in the staircases of almost all the houses here at the end of the winter. On the ground floor, I take a look over the banisters and discover my flashlight. I walk down, picking it up from the basement stairs and switching it on. In the cone of light I find the fallen hook, a dark brown plastic coat peg. I run a finger over the dry adhesive surface, slip it in my pocket and put the light back down on the ground.

On my way out to the street I brush against the fence to the next-door building. The hungry cat has had an abundant scavenging session on the other side of the wire mesh. It's tipped over two garbage sacks, ripped them open and disembowelled them. Rifled for edible elements, the entire trash is lying scattered on the ground: yogurt pots, vegetable peelings, socks and aluminium foil, empty tuna cans, tampons and the remains of a pasta dish. In the fence hangs a nest of teabags, dunked in a quark-like substance and knotted together, and a paper napkin flatters above the drain, covered with the shells of beheaded boiled eggs.

The door to the side wing of Number Fifteen opens. A thin man comes out of the building, dressed in a fake

leather jacket and granite-coloured boots. He rests his
shopping bag on the ground and puts on a hat with
earflaps folded upward, throwing an angry look at the
garbage. Then he spots me behind the fence. I walk into
the front building and up one flight of stairs, waiting.

A little later I hear the front door and see him walking in. He looks up but doesn't see me and carries on to
the yard. I head downstairs again, peering cautiously
around the corner of the wall. The man goes into the
side wing but comes straight out again. He obviously
doesn't feel like looking for me in the empty building.
He catches sight of the construction company sign. He
stops, reads it and taps at it. Then he walks back out to
the street with fast strides.

On my way back from the bakery, where I gave a fin-
gernail-chewing shop assistant with carrot-red hair and
a diamond stud in her temple a two-hundred-mark note
to pay for the bread rolls, I come across the remnants of
the garbage bags in the yard, two empty grey sacks dangling from the wire fence. The man with the hat must
have thrown them over from Number Fifteen. They're
not mine. Mine are green and they're carefully stowed
away in the containers.

I take a step closer, releasing the plastic from the
mesh. A booklet is suspended in the remains of the bags,
half slipped out of the hole torn by cat's claws below the
knotted top. I take it out and turn it over. The cardboard

binding is covered in green cloth. A ribbon drawn through two gaps closes the book with a bow, next to it an adhesive nametag with two lines of smudged children's handwriting. The book belongs to Dunkel.

I lift it up, blowing off crumbs and dirt and stowing it under my jacket. I pick up the sacks, dragging them behind me onto the street to the entrance to Number Fifteen. They've added a number code to the lock on the front door but it must have been cracked. The keypad is hanging on loose wires, ripped from its anchoring next to the door handle. I open up and drag the bags into next door's yard. Once there, I open a trash can and throw them in.

Strange to see my own house from the other side of the fence. It looks so tall and brittle with its outer walls dotted with remains of plaster, the grey-speckled roof covered in pigeon droppings down to the gutters, with its drooping aerial cables and the broken panes of the windows, their jagged holes without reflections pointing into the darkness of abandoned homes.

On the way back to my apartment, I stop between the two flights of stairs before I reach the top floor. On the side facing the front of the building is a board door to the outside toilet. There's another door on the same level on my side. When you open it, though, all that's behind it is a broom cupboard, complete with a sink, buckets and balding brushes. With the aid of an iron wire bent into a hook, I first gained entry to Dunkel's smallest room shortly before I moved in, just as I still do today. Silently tolerated by my neighbour, not leaving a trace.

Dunkel's antipathy for redecorating comes into its own here. The walls of the small room are painted the same colour as the doors, glossy grey. The intact paint forms a conspicuous contrast to the tiny rotten window, its frame having adopted the texture of driftwood through decades of exposure to the weather. Only in the cracks do stubborn paint remnants cling on, like grooves of dirt in an old cake of soap. A hook riveted to plywood is fastened to the wall, where Dunkel hangs rolls of violet paper that give off a faint scent. She has laid a pile of comics next to the bend in the pipe.

I lock myself in, sitting down on the thin plastic lid that slips to one side at the slightest movement, open my jacket, and the booklet falls onto my lap. I unfasten the ribbon. *Poetry Album* is written in royal-blue left-leaning handwriting on the inside of the binding — Poetry Album, Bad Homburg, a street name and Dunkel's name.

Bad Homburg.

Pedestrian zones, spas, double garages.

I press my fists against my forehead, breathing downward, pressing my feet into a firm stand with their entire soles. Spilt liquid has seeped into the inside of the book via the open edges, clotting the paper together into crackly rind. I attempt to turn the pages, my heart beating loud and painful. Cautiously, I peel off each strip of adhesive page, scratching my way through faded felt-pen flowers, wooden calligraphy and multicoloured underlinings, through stickers of cats, angels, puppies and through the ornate initial letters of lines of verse. With every layer I reveal, it's not my doubt that grows but more and more the certainty of finding März, any moment now, behind the next page or the one after that.

> When the rivers flow uphill,
> And the rabbits hunters kill,
> When the water doesn't wet you,
> Only then will I forget you.

Written diagonally across the top third of the page, without a date.

14

I leave the police station around noon and walk back home to Weigandufer. In the left-hand outer pocket of my cardigan is the little card Wang gave me before she left the waiting room, holding her daughter by the hand. A black, slightly spotted copy on stiff dark red paper, cut down to business card size. A name and an address in the district of Wedding in small capitals, below four large, sweeping characters.

I carry the card in my cardigan pocket all summer long. It gets hot. The cold inside me remains; I rarely leave the house without my cardigan.

At the end of June I move into the small, bare balcony room where my flatmate has left behind a broken black-and-white television and a large foam mattress. I gather together a few items of clothing, covers and papers, lock my room and set myself up in there.

The warm season drags by, disintegrating into meaningless days.

I unplug the telephone, apply for orphan's benefit, avoid all contact. Once a week I go shopping at the nearest supermarket, piling my supplies in a shady corner of the balcony. Some days my life seems to stretch from the door of the room to the walls of the balcony, on others only to the edges of the mattress. Now and then it ends at the point where my body reaches the extent of its physical dimensions. I sense it might be possible to minimize myself even more, inwardly, but at that point I'm overcome with fear and I get up out of bed. I get dressed, empty the chamber pot next to the unused electric heater, force myself out onto the street and the green verges alongside the canal, occasionally cooking, tidying and beginning my withdrawal anew.

I have to start over from the beginning with seeing and hearing. I have to learn it all over again. Up to now I've been too imprecise about it, not conscientious enough. I overtaxed myself with too many unnecessary impressions. Now I spend several hours of every day looking at a square of woodchip-papered wall. Or I study the course of the skirting boards, the irregular lines of the gaps between the floorboards, the sound of car tyres on wet street, doors slamming, footsteps, dogs barking on the stairs. Once a week someone comes to clean the staircase, and then I know it's a Tuesday. I hear the wiping movements, the bang of the broom on the edges of the steps, the cleaning lady's cracking and rustling bending movements. Occasionally someone rings my doorbell but I don't open up.

In September I discover that the television does work after all.

On the way back inside from the balcony, I come across a socket previously hidden by the TV. The plug has been pulled partway out. It's stuck, as if someone has only just tugged at it, with a child safety tab torn from its anchors in the socket. I remove the tab and reinsert the plug. Curious now, I press the ON button. The screen lights up with a chirping sound. From the centre of the screen, a dot of light gradually extends to the edges, withdrawing to half its size again and casting hints of a picture that spreads out and straightens up.

I gaze into the face of a newsreader. The reception is faultless. She's sitting at a desk with papers in her hand, next to a square showing varying images, a photo of a cornfield, a rapeseed field, a smelting plant. The woman pinches her sheets of paper between her fingers, reading out statistics and units. Four hundred and seventy-one thousand, eight hundred and thirty-three tonnes. Twelve point three nine per cent. Fifty thousand, two hundred and sixty-seven hectares.

I throw myself onto the bed, tip grains of packet soup into the electric kettle and stir with the shaft of a knife. I haven't watched TV for years. The last time was at my parents' place, where these East German channels weren't even tuned in. As lukewarm soupy liquid runs through the spout into my mouth, I follow party meetings, the presentation of greetings between brother nations, the weather report. Then I put the kettle on the floor at my side, pull the set closer up to the edge of the mattress, and press more buttons.

The next channels are driven snow. Only the last button offers another picture, broadcasting unfocused, badly shaded contours to a fast-talking male voice that breaks off occasionally, reverting to interference.

The aerial is a tangle of cables wrapped around a strangely shaped metal structure that ends in an ivory-coloured plastic foot. Cautiously, I move it to and fro and shake it, but there's no change to the picture. As I lift it up the picture disappears entirely, but when I tug at the wires it seems clearer for a moment. I take the knife I used to stir my soup, insert the shaft between two floorboards, wedge the cable into a knothole in the floor along with the slimmer blade, place the aerial back on the television set with its cable now taut, and weigh the whole thing down with two packs of long-life milk.

Shadowy double edges are still drifting to the right of the contours and there's a slight fuzz beneath the speaker's voice. But the reception gets clearer now. I see a large house with a garden, surrounded by a high fence. The camera zooms in on the entrance sign. An embassy building, in front of it loosely scattered groups of people, some in uniform. The commentator's voice imitates agitation. The whole building is full of people; they've spread out around the house and set up tents in the grounds. Some of them give interviews. They're sitting on their worldly goods, on sacks, bags and clothes, as if they had to protect the last remnants of their old lives against the new life to come through physical contact with their bodies.

Now I switch on the TV every evening.

I see some scenes several times over. Two little children playing with a tower of empty drinks crates at the foot of the one of the entrance pillars, and a woman with bobbing gold earrings and a leather jacket sewn together out of countless pieces, laid loosely around her shoulders. She's standing outside a tent talking into the microphone, and she can't keep her hands away from her mouth. Over and over, she strokes rapid, ordering fingers around her chin and the corners of her lips, as if that might put a brake on the words slipping out of her, smooth them out, if necessary propel them quickly back into her mouth.

A few days later, they let the people leave the country. The reception is particularly bad that evening. I can only vaguely make out the barricaded train arriving on the platform of the border town. Heads appear at torn-open windows. A dancing, unfocused pale garland forms, presumably a row of waving hands urging toward a second row of waving positioned on the platform and heading for the train. On the opposing channel, freshly polished machinery lined up on a collective farm. Then comes a tracking shot over the Müggelsee lake, where the reed-lined banks are already glowing in autumnal colours. And then there's a sound—not a bang, not a slam; more like a crunch as if thin glass were being ground—and my picture is gone.

Stunned, I stare at the now dull screen. I get up, walking over to the TV and knocking at it, but nothing happens. I pace around the room a few times, indignant. I inspect the casing from the back but can't make anything out. But I have to do something, I think; I ought to unscrew the damn thing, perhaps the tube has burnt out, perhaps I can get a replacement part.

In search of a screwdriver, I end up in my old room. I press down the door handle and enter. It's cool, with a slight trace of dust on top of everything. I squat and begin rummaging in tins, cupboards, drawers and in suitcases under the bed.

I don't give up my search until the middle of the night, amid a chaos of rifled objects. I take a triple socket and extension lead with me, but even as I'm standing in the doorway I've forgotten what I wanted them for. On my way out I cast a glance at my former desk. There's the leather pouch and the two pipes. Picking up the foreign objects, I leave the room and close the door.

The next day I go out on the balcony. I lay the objects in the empty space on the balcony rim with its vacant double wall for pot plants, unfold a wooden garden chair tanned by the weather and standing in a corner among broken saucers, jam jars, clay pots part-piled, part-filled with parched earth and grey stalks, and a cloth bag of plastic clothes pegs, and sit down.

I lay the pipes on the palm of my hand. They are two plain, deer-brown wooden pipes with black mouth-pieces chewed where the smoke comes out. I look at them until dusk, then I put them and the pouch in one of the empty flower pots and make my way back inside.

From now on I go out on the balcony every day. It's grown cool outside, autumnal. I look out over the roofs of my street, where the houses first grow lower to the east and then give way to an allotment garden. I let the soft wood of the pipes slip through my fingers, watching the sun go down above the roofs of the neighbouring buildings, over the red-brown façade of a film copying works, over trimmed hedges, apple trees and mesh fences.

At the end of October I go down to the ground floor, where a tiny store provides the neighbours with their basic needs; a mixture of lottery tickets, drinks, cheap toys and newspapers. I buy a large cigarette lighter where the flame comes out at the side, plus a tamper and a set of wire pipe cleaners.

Upstairs again, I step straight onto the balcony, placing my purchases next to the pipes, pick one of them up and put it to my lips. My tongue accidentally touches the mouthpiece. The unexpectedly bitter taste sends saliva shooting into my mouth. Disgusted, I open my lips wide and the pipe falls on my lap.

The following day, I take the half-filled tobacco pouch in my hand and begin to pack one of the pipes. The pouch is made of greasy leather in the shape of an ancient hand axe. A picture is stamped into the leather on one side, its colour faded but the texture still preserved. It depicts two parachutists soaring earthward like stones with their limbs bent, at the precise moment when their parachutes have opened but they haven't fallen far enough for the lines to take their weight. Underneath them in a semi-circle are the words: *Parachutistes de la legion étrangère.*

My first attempts at smoking are pathetic.

The pipes are either too loosely or too tightly packed. Saliva and tobacco juice pool in the shaft. The burning shag tastes spicy and either glows hot immediately or smoulders with difficulty. The clouds rising from the pipe bowl make my eyes water. I accidentally inhale a lungful, making me cough for days, but I don't give up; I keep trying. November comes, and still I sit on the balcony in my cardigan every evening.

I know now that I have to take even drags, and I mustn't breathe in the smoke. It's best to look down at the street indifferently, not thinking at all about the pipe in my mouth, starting with loosely packed tobacco and adding more from time to time. I like following the loops of smoke at the end of the pipe with my eyes until they lose themselves in the air. Sometimes I can watch them drifting all the way to the middle of the street. On windy days the smoke is blown in all directions, right from the bowl. The calm days are particularly pleasant; it looks as if the grey-blue veils were seeking their own path through the air in absolute peace.

And then they come. Suddenly, on a day in November, they come.

I was prepared. I always read the newspaper headlines on the boards down at the shop. For the first time in ages, I laughed out loud and looked at passers-by as they walked along, almost even speaking to someone. Later I simply sat on my balcony as usual.

And now they come.

I turn onto my street from the supermarket, holding a shopping basket in my hand. From the dead end near the border, they come walking toward me in small groups. From time to time they stop and look up at the facades. The first of them cross the street, spot the sign of the store I've just left behind me, and surround me at the narrow gateway leading to the entrance and the parking spaces. They stare at my basket. I'm hemmed in by strangers, all of them looking at what I've bought. Rice and packet soup, wine and paper tissues, peppers and liquid soap, canned drinks, chocolate biscuits, yogurt and cold meat sealed in plastic. Some of them are so close to me that their shoulders almost brush against me, but they seem to take absolutely no notice of me.

They're looking at the food, entirely occupied with themselves or with the thought of the possible purchase or consumption of these items.

I drop my shopping and run down the road. I don't turn around again until I reach the patch of grass leading to the bridge. A minor bottleneck has formed around my basket, which is blocking the entrance and still being inspected by the people flowing in, yet nobody moves it. The people skip over it or climb past it at the side, not surprised at this hurdle, and nobody has stopped to watch me leave.

The idea of fetching my supplies, entangling myself all over again in the apathetically staring mob or even walking home along the pavements as they get more and more crowded, is unbearable. I continue along the canal, still in the direction of my escape. Across the bridge, alongside bars, a school and a church, past the town hall flowerbeds, a pharmacy, the bus shelter and across the traffic lights to the escalator. The northbound underground train is at the platform. The man in blue throws me a challenging look. I take three paces into the nearest, almost empty carriage and collapse onto the green seat, cooling the back of my head on the window pane and closing my eyes before I glide into the tunnel.

15

Eight stairs.

The door to Dunkel's flat is still open. She has fixed a wire basket using plastic tape under the inside of the letter-slit, for the post to fall into. The basket has come unattached at one corner, hanging loose and rattling to and fro in the draught blowing in from her windows.

I climb the steps slowly, not looking at the stairs or at my feet, my eyes fixed on the wall ahead, on the light switch that hasn't worked for a long time, a doubly framed square with a round button at the centre, hanging on the wall between the two entrances.

My door is ajar. I walk quietly down the empty hall, the green book cradled in my right arm, the paper bag of bread rolls in the other.

The snoring has stopped.

I go into the kitchen, put the bag on the table, step up to the sink and turn on the tap. Water hits the steel surface of the sink in arrhythmic thrusts, making a throbbing sound. I turn the tap down slightly and the flow of water falters, the sound growing louder. I want März to wake up. I fill the kettle, slam it down on the gas hob and begin humming tunelessly to myself.

I watched him for a long time earlier; I'm shocked at the effort sleeping seems to cost him. His body tosses restlessly to and fro on the bed, as if to cast off shackles. His mouth open wide, he lies there and gasps for air at irregular intervals, as if constantly about to suffocate, and the creases aren't smoothed in his sleep-contorted features; they are even more entrenched.

Breakfast is ready. Butter, honey, quark, tea and the rolls. I pile everything onto a tray and wedge the green book into a gap between the teapot and the edge of the tray. Then I sit down on the kitchen chair and pour myself a tea. I down it in fast gulps, pour another cup, drink that. In between I listen carefully, but there's not a sound to be heard from the next room.

I give up after the third cup. I get up and walk down the hall to my room with the tray in my hands.

He's sitting there.

The bed is made. The covers are folded and rolled up behind his back. März is sitting on the mat with his legs crossed, blinking at me with a drowsy, sleep-thickened look on his face. He's clutching something in his fingers. It spins on a string, wraps itself around his wrist, slapping into his arm. Now März swings his hand in the opposite direction. The object unwinds and flies in circles, getting larger and larger and then decreasing again until it hits his arm over again. Confused, I watch that arm, now swinging for the third time. März opens his hand, letting go of the thread. His projectile flies straight across the room at me, knocking over the second, still dry cup on the tray and falling in the sugar bowl. Two parachutists land head-over-heels in the white sand.

'Where did you get this from?'

'Found it. I found it in a disused station. Why?'

'It reminds me of a friend of mine. He used to run around with a leather pouch on a string round his neck. He was French. No, actually he was Basque.'

März runs a hand through his hair, laughs, and reaches for the cups and plates.

'I met him at a petrol station. Just outside Marseille. I was seventeen, hitchhiking round France. He more or less lived on the street. We stayed together for five weeks, travelling all across France. Total freedom. That's not something you experience every day. You have to break your boundaries to be free.'

'You think so?'

I take the knife, butter two halves of a roll and hold one up. He nods and I put it on his plate.

'I took him home with me when the school holidays were over.'

'To your parents?'

'Yeah. I can still remember my old man's look of amazement when we came strolling along the path outside his garden. Unwashed. Stoned. Me with my backpack, my friend with this old sports bag with an ad for some French beer company on it. The old man saw us coming through the living room windows, huge French windows that got cleaned once a week and were always sparkling. There he stood, his cup of coffee in his hand, and all around him were reflections in the window of his sheep . . .'

'Sheep?'

'My old man keeps sheep as a hobby. He has a paddock right outside the house. The sheep were standing at the fence and staring when we arrived. We pointed at the huge window and pissed ourselves laughing. Then we went inside and I thought, that's it, we've messed it up. But I was wrong; he let my friend stay for the time being.'

'That was nice of your stepfather then, wasn't it?'

März's eyes flash an irritated look at me.

'Four bedrooms, three bathrooms. We had more than enough space in the house.'

He bites into his roll and chews, looking at the leather pouch and his cup, bites again, chews, swallows and shakes his head with emphasis.

'Sometimes, when my old man knew you liked something, he'd let you keep it to begin with. Until you got really attached to it. And then he'd take it away from you again. Out of pure cruelty, just so it really hurt.'

'And that's what happened with your friend?'

'That's right. He stayed with us for two months. I took him everywhere with me—to school, to friends, to rugby matches. But a few weeks later the problems started.'

'Your father didn't like him.'

'At first he put up with more than I'd thought he would. Stealing for example. He'd never have let me get away with that. When he found out I thought he'd throw him out on his ear, but my old man had to play the social worker number. He let him work in the garden and stuff like that.'

März shoves the second half of his roll in his mouth and lowers his head, his fingers sweeping a pile of crumbs on the mat into parallel lines. He looks at them and brushes them together again with the ball of his hand.

'Then the guy fell for my sister. He kept chasing her round—it even got on my nerves. But that wasn't it. That wasn't the reason why he chucked him out. It was because of the sheep.'

'The sheep?'

'The old man was castrating lambs. We were supposed to help him. There are these rubber rings for it, you put them over the males' dicks. We held onto the sheep, and the old man put the rubber rings on them. He must have not realized until later what he'd actually been doing, what the rubber things were used for, not until the next day. Then he went out to the herd and pulled the rings off again. They screamed in pain. You could hear it right across the estate. My old man flipped out when he came home. First he called the vet and then he made my friend pack his things. He bundled him into the car and me along with him. Then we abandoned him. At a motorway service station between Frankfurt and Kassel. Like some dog you don't want any more. He watched me as we drove away. He didn't say anything, didn't do anything, he just looked at me. I've never forgotten that look.'

'Did you ever see him again?'

März shakes his head.

'I got the occasional postcard. From Freiburg, Cologne, Bremen. He couldn't go back to France because he was on the wanted list there.'

März takes a deep breath.

'He came to Berlin after the Wall came down.'

'Is he here now, in town?'

'Yes, and I'm going to meet him. I still owe him, and now I can pay him back.'

März leans back and pats at his backpack. Then he grins at me, looking pensively at the leather bundle in the sugar bowl.

'Do you know what this means?'

He takes the pouch out of the bowl and holds the time-faded print up to my eyes. März's index finger is chewed out of joint on the side facing his thumb, his nail almost twice as wide as the lettering he runs it along, slowly spelling out the words.

'Parachutistes. That's clear enough.'

'. . . it was a pouch just like this? With the same writing, the men jumping . . . ?'

I feel a sudden heat.

'Yes. And this here means foreign legion. Parachutists of the foreign legion. He claimed he was there once, really wanted to learn how to parachute, but they wouldn't take him. He was too short.'

'Too short?'

I croak. My rational mind shouts coincidence, a stupid, meaningless, idiotic coincidence, but I start feeling hotter and hotter, sweat forming patches on my back. My feet feel swollen, my hands too.

'. . . he's a pretty small man, maybe five feet three. I didn't believe the thing about the foreign legion though. That was rubbish. A bunch of military freaks—he'd never have fitted in.'

'When are you meeting him?'

März looks up. The distorted tone in my voice catches his attention.

'This evening.'

He shifts away from me, rubbing his chin with his knuckles.

'Why do you want to know?'

I try to give my voice solidity, focusing on a point in between his eyebrows.

'I want to come with you.'

'No way.'

März gets restless. He pulls his tobacco out of his shirt pocket and releases the sticky tape. A couple of white cigarette filters fall out, rolling down his knees.

'No, really. It's between him and me.'

I bite my lips, staring at the streaks in my cold tea.

'You have to understand,' März starts again, 'I'm glad to have found him. I don't know what state he's in now, nearly ten years later, and I haven't told him about the money thing yet. And anyway I've already dragged you much too far into the whole thing . . .'

I get up, put the crockery on the tray, push the tray in front of the stove, shake my hands and feet. Then I sit down again, wrapping my arms around my legs and laying my chin in the indentation between my knees.

'I know how to find your father. I know where the factory is where he used to work.'

März's mouth jerks open and he drops his tobacco, the rolled cigarette sticking to his lower lip. His right hand conceals the lighter, clutched tightly. He raises his hand to his face, holding a flame to the tip of his cigarette. I pull a face, which he ignores, but I don't say anything. März inhales, blowing the smoke downward out of his nostrils.

'Where?' he whispers.

'I'll only tell you if you take me with you.'

'What do you want from him?'

'I want to give him the pouch. And the pipes.'

'You mean . . . ?'

'Yes.'

'You can give them to me.'

'No.'

'Why not?'

I bend forward and take the cigarette out of März's mouth. His lips grow soft. For a moment I feel like kissing them. I hold the cigarette between my finger and thumb and take a long drag before I answer him, expelling the words and the smoke simultaneously.

'It's between him and me.'

16

The suburban line heading out to the southeast is a cord of tracks along grey plant skeletons, weeds growing between the grid of rails, points and signals. We pass corrugated iron barracks and abandoned factories, covered in giant blue and silver letters, a block of identical housing estates dulled by smog in the distance, piles of coal and rubble and a slim ribbon of allotments directly alongside the railway embankment.

New office buildings pop up occasionally between demolished gaps and the ailing walls of residential buildings. So shiny, so perfect that it doesn't look as if they had foundations here; more as if they came from far away, landed on a planet of sand, soot, ruins and graffiti.

März cranes his neck for the next station sign.

'Baumschulenweg. Ours is the next stop.'

'I know.'

We're sitting sideways-on in one of the new red suburban trains. Leaning into the corner, his feet in his mustard-coloured boots resting against a pole, März is working away at his ticket. He tatters it in all directions, folding it up into rectangular parcels and unfolding it again. He shapes it into a tube, bends it, rolls the pink paper between his hands until it forms a ball, finally squashing the ball between finger and thumb and depositing it in his cord trousers. I undo my jacket, pulling the green book out of my inside pocket.

'Does this look familiar?'

März shakes his head.

'What is it?'

'It belongs to Dunkel. I found it out in the yard. It's a poetry album.'

'A what?'

'A poetry album. You're in there too.'

I push the book toward him, flicking it open for him.

He looks at the page for a moment and laughs.

'So I am.'

I wait for him to say something else. Something out of all the things I don't know. But März presses ribs into the plastic of the seat back with the nail of his right-hand little finger, silent.

We cross a canal branching off from the river Spree and leave the city proper. Beyond the water begin low warehouses, administrative buildings, car parks. Set against a silhouette of steaming chimneys, an old brewery building approaches and next to us, on the margins of a freight station, begin the grounds of a liquid gas factory with rows of different coloured metal cylinders.

März has stood up. His hand is on the door even before the train enters the station. He presses the button at short intervals, coaxing hissing sounds from the blocked opening mechanism. The door slides open while the train is still moving. März topples forward, stumbles but regains his balance with a leap onto the platform.

The station building is tiled in lime green, unpleasantly lit and dirty, and leads directly to the tram stops with no forecourt.

We walk to the pedestrian underpass, a low-roofed tunnel with mosaics on the walls taking us to the other side of the street. März walks closely along one side, his jacket swiping against highly polished walls. A tram thunders above our heads. As we climb the steps back up, we see it disappearing toward the bridge over the Spree—an ancient, dented single carriage.

A few minutes later we're at the river. I step onto the bridge, pulling März closer to me, waving a hand at dirty yellow buildings behind landing stages.

März throws me a look of annoyance. He looks exhausted; he's sweating. His trousers are wrinkled with creases, dried saliva in the corners of his mouth. Every few paces, he tugs the carrying straps of his backpack and gives a skip to bring his luggage into the right position.

One of the tin trams overtakes us as we're crossing the bridge. It brakes with a buzzing sound at the stop. A poorly dressed man with chin-length hair levers the door open and gets on. The dented vehicle gives off a shrill ring, rumbling on at walking pace along window-less industrial buildings, behind which it turns right with a screech. We follow the tracks to a crossroads, cobbled with roughly hewn stones framing a tangle of tram tracks leading in different directions, some opening onto dead ends.

März stops. He points at a road leading upriver, where the tracks end embedded in the tar of the street only a few metres on.

'That's the direction we came from, Dunkel and I. But not across this bridge here—it was that one over there.'

I nod and gesture in the other direction with my head.

Beneath a web of low-hanging overhead tram cables, we leave the bridge, cross at the crossroads and turn into a strangely halved street.

It's the one I saw in the photo. Little seems to have changed here over the past few decades. The street leads along Prussian factories blocking the view of the Spree, the tracks of the works tram running parallel. On the other side are tenement buildings, built in the style of their inner-city cousins but one or two storeys lower. On their ground floors, shop windows line up after shop windows, the high street of a residential area built directly next to the factory chimneys.

Many of the buildings are vacant. The windows are nailed shut with crossed planks, the entrances bricked up.

März drags his right hand along a railing at the edge of the pavement. He looks behind him from time to time as if someone might be following him, here of all places. The cable works must be coming any minute now, it might be the next factory gates or the next but one. A silent März walks at my side. His mood seems to darken with every step, his face closing up more and more.

People are coming toward us. They've come out of a supermarket lit up in red and white, set slightly back from the street, and turn onto more occupied side streets. They're pulling little trolleys behind them or holding long-handled bags; some of them have small black cases stuffed with shopping, the kind that men use to take thermos flasks and sandwiches to work—but these people aren't in work; they look poor, aimless and tired. Trams roll past them at close intervals, most of their carriages empty.

We cross the street. A side road leading toward the river ends a few yards in at a mesh fence. Behind it, between barrels, containers and diagonally parked trucks, I spot the first cable drums and the factory entrance, a gate guarded by a doorman next to a glass display case.

März slows his pace. He lifts the backpack off his shoulder, reaches into his inside pocket and takes out the photo, re-shouldering the backpack and catching me up at the gate.

I glance at the display case. A newspaper cutting is pinned to the back wall. A factory floor filled with men in dark suits, between them the Queen of England, a handbag dangling from her lower arm and an angular hat perched on her hair.

März presses the photo into my hand. His silver-ringed hands are trembling.

I step up to the gatekeeper's cabin, push the picture through an open flap at mouth level and indicate the face with the cross above it. The man behind the counter raises his grey-stubbled chin, takes a glance at it and shakes his head, handing me back the photo.

'We've come specially from West Germany to find him.'

The gatekeeper gestures across the road.

'Ask the landlord over there. He knows everyone round here.'

I nod, thanking him, and turn back to März standing waiting at the barrier. He's pulled a blue cord out of the hem of his hood and is chewing at it.

'Okay, let's go.'

We cross the street, reaching the bar in a few paces. A menu written in felt-tip pen, faded almost to illegibility by the light, is on display next to the door.

März opens the handle and we enter.

The inside of the bar is surprisingly bright. We look around at whitewashed walls that must have been painted not all that long ago, nicotine-yellow already in the corners. The tables and chairs are pale brown and glossy like hot fat. Close to the counter hangs an electronic dartboard, next to it a glass-fronted cabinet containing bundles of darts with cardboard labels.

We take a seat at a table by the window. Not much later the waitress, a woman with black hair, pallid skin and a broad-striped blouse, brings us two glasses of apple juice.

I drink. März twists his glass to and fro on the damp cardboard coaster, his index finger boring into a burn mark on the tablecloth. The landlord comes out from a side room behind the counter—a stocky, short-armed man in horn-rimmed spectacles and a checked polo shirt. März leaps up, walking over to show him the picture.

A glass of Coke in his hand, the landlord joins us at our table, shifting a chair into position, sitting down and laying his hands and the photo on the tabletop. Then he extracts a packet of cigarettes from his pocket, strokes it smooth and turns the opened packet to offer us one.

We decline. März pulls out his lighter.

'What do you want the man for?'

A brief silence. März clears his throat.

'He's my father.'

The fruit machine emits a chirrup.

Ten minutes later we're standing on the right street, a short, store-free link between the factories and the grounds of a coal yard. Most of the buildings aren't painted but they look inhabited. Number Three is a grey house with foot-sized balconies. The front door is locked, the bell system new. März's father's name is listed under ground floor, rear building.

März holds his finger on the button. We wait, the intercom remaining silent and the door not opening. März tries a second time, in vain.

The old carriage entrance to one side is open.

A mountain of junk is piled up in the yard, its tip extending to the second storey, windows ajar.

A baby starts crying.

März drums at the ground-floor window. Two panes are blocked by cacti, at the third hangs a dwarf made of dough, fastened on a length of wool. The baby launches into a rhythmically interrupted, still hesitant whimpering, which soon rises to a commanding volume. A rusty squeaking sound mingles with its tones, sounding mechanical rather than human.

I hold my hands to my ears and step up to a hole in the fence. The squeaking gets louder.

A path on the other side of the fence leads past the rear building. I bend down, creeping through the hole in the wire mesh, and walk along the side wall. A small overgrown garden begins behind the house.

The unkempt grass dotted with stinging nettles is knee-high at the edges and trampled flat at the centre. There's a sandpit nailed together out of boards and a tall wooden frame. On one side of the frame dangle ragged climbing ropes, on the other an old man is sitting on a swing.

He's wearing rubber boots and a yellow raincoat and swinging to and fro with loud squeaks. The hood only barely covers his pale strands of hair. Drops of water run down the sharp creases between his nose and mouth, dripping from his shoulders onto his hands.

I can't tell whether his eyes are green; just that he hasn't noticed me even though I'm clearly visible at the entrance to the garden. His left arm, hooked around the squeaking chain of the swing, is hugging a bottle.

I beat a retreat.

Two cautious backward steps, a turn, two jumps, then I'm creeping through the fence. März is sheltering in the entrance, his teeth chattering. He sees me coming and turns to leave.

'Wait. He's back there in the garden. Go through the fence, I'll stay here.'

März's eyes widen; reddened, tired eyes staring at me in disbelief. Until I say, 'Go on, off you go,' almost shouting. 'It's OK, I'll wait for you, just get on with it.'

März keeps looking at me even as he's in motion. I can see him aging in that look. He stumbles sideways, his face still fixed on me, the wet making his furrows stand out all the more, and with every yard he moves closer to the fence his shoulders droop lower, as if burdened by tons of luggage too heavy to actually carry.

Now he's reached the fence and bends down.

There's a bang.

An angry opening of the balcony door directly above me, and the baby's screams are suddenly louder. Someone pushes the child outside in its pram. Then the balcony door is shut again with a second bang.

I turn my head away and hope März has finally stopped looking at me. The baby screams incessantly. I stare at the pile of junk, counting to fifty. The screaming gets throaty, desperate, hoarse.

März has got his backpack trapped in the fence. He makes an angry lurch forward, landing in the dirt on the other side of the opening. His jacket is torn at the shoulder. A handful of white feathers sail over the wire mesh. I lean on the wall of the entrance, still counting, to a hundred, to two hundred and on and on.

The baby stops screaming.

I see März coming toward me. He's walking fast, his eyes wet. I go to meet him, opening my arms. He bats them away, walking out onto the street. Outside, he throws his backpack on the pavement and takes out a thick wedge of hundreds. His hands full of banknotes, he goes through the letterboxes mounted on the wall, finds the right one and stuffs the notes through the slot. Then he wipes his face, grabs my hand, shouts, 'Let's get out of here,' and tugs me to the main road at a jog.

A tram approaches from the distance. We reach the stop before it arrives. The metal carriage halts and we rattle at the door handle, climbing ladder-like steps and collapsing onto the nearest seats.

März wraps his arms around his backpack and buries his head in the fabric. His shoulders twitch. He has hooked his thumbs into two leather loops, bending them until the seams almost rip.

17

I open my eyes and look up at a square of laminated plastic the size of a credit card wedged into a woman's hand, printed in black and yellow with a colour-copied passport photo and a hole with a chain through it at the top right-hand corner.

The train brakes with a screech. A curve, and now it begins its crawl through the first of the six ghost stations. I'm sitting with my back to the platform, the tiles of Heinrich-Heine-Strasse station pushing past the windows, in front of them the head of a woman in her early fifties bending down to me, dressed in a cotton sweater with a complicated pattern, a cream beret and a black patent raincoat.

'Well, young lady, what's up?'

Blinking, I shove my hands into my jacket pockets, feeling only fluff and seams, on the right my key and a card—which I tug out and hold up.

'No, that's no use to me. You come with us next stop.'

The carriage is almost empty. A second, younger woman in a tracksuit approaches from the aisle, the handles of a large shopping bag slipping from her shoulder to her elbow. She reaches into the bag and whips out a clipboard with forms attached.

'Got any ID?'

The woman in the raincoat hands me back the business card.

'Kung fu! Never had that one before.'

I pull my wallet out of my trousers and place my ID card on the clipboard. The younger woman copies down my details.

'Get yourself a ticket at Voltastrasse if you want to continue your journey.'

They give me a bank debit slip to pay my fine and withdraw to the other end of the carriage. I turn aside and hold my face against the window until it stops feeling red and upset. Rosenthaler Platz station. The train rolls through dust-coated orange. The cabins on the platforms have viewing slits and are brightly lit. Sometimes you can make out sections of uniform behind these windows: cap visors, epaulettes or rifle barrels lurching into view for a few moments.

The next station but one is clean and busy. I get off the train. The platform cabin has large windows, a Turkish-run kiosk. The conductor mumbles words into a microphone on a wooden platform, seeing off the train. I buy juice and a pastry at the counter, sitting down on a bench and revolving the card between my finger and thumb by its long edges. *Chinese Kung Fu with Wang Ying.* I unscrew the cap of the juice bottle, stuff the pastry into my mouth, drink and chew as I walk, jogging up the stairs to the centre of Brunnenstrasse and crossing it with three leaps, through dense afternoon traffic almost at a standstill.

Wind chases leaves into the entrances of the modern residential blocks, penetrating through the weave of my jacket sleeves. After a short walk, I reach the street printed on the card. The house is an unadorned old building with peeling white paint. Saws from a carpentry workshop screech in the first courtyard. The passage to the second yard is blocked by a caravan. Under the expressionless gaze of a bearded carpenter, I ease past its sides to the very rear building, a two-storey former factory.

The front door isn't locked. Behind the stairs I find an entrance, with no doorbell or sign. I step up to the door, pressing an ear to the frame, and hear voices, slams and a slight dragging sound.

Before I've even decided to knock the door is flung open, inward. I stumble forward, standing close before a small, muscular man in baggy black trousers and a ribbed vest. He grins at me, skipping from one foot to another in a pleased and rather fidgety manner, and asks me in by touching my shoulder.

We enter a hall extending across the entire half of the ground floor. There's a smell of rubber and spices, the large space empty but for a pile of gymnastics mats against the opposite wall. A chubby teenager in a sleeveless jacket with patch pockets drags a mat right across the room, hoists it above his head and throws it on the pile. An older man in a faded black Chinese suit is standing at the window, drinking from a can of lemonade and opening the uppermost of a row of looped buttons at his neck. Then he puts the can down on the windowsill, walks to the opposing wall and launches into a rapid series of kicks at the sand bag dangling from the ceiling.

The man who opened the door to me gestures at a shelf lined with shoes. I slip my own off and add them. On stockinged feet, I follow him right across the hall, where fabric hung on rods and embroidered with fringes and characters is attached to the walls. Behind it we enter a windowless room. I go inside, sit down and wait.

The room is long and narrow, painted yellow and furnished with white benches, clothes hooks and a large desk discarded from an office. On the wall above the table is a poster from the Peking tourism office, showing the Great Wall of China snaking toward a sunset. Two urn-shaped trophies are displayed on the top shelf of a black-stained cabinet, alongside them cases containing medallions decorated with characters, embedded in hollows of artificial velvet. Next to the second door is a basin surrounded by toothbrushes, bottles and tubes, beneath tiles covered in splashes. Two folding beds are pushed into the niche behind it.

Wang's daughter comes in. She greets me with an earnest nod. I can't tell whether she recognizes me. With rapid motions, as if she had to take up an abandoned post immediately, she clambers onto the chair at the desk, adjusts a lamp clipped to it, switches it on and takes the top exercise book from a pile. She folds open a rough page printed with red boxes and begins to fill the boxes with lines and ticks.

Now Wang comes toward us, walking across the hall. I know it's her before I've even seen her face properly; I can tell her by her agile movements. She enters the cloakroom and looks at me. It only takes her a few seconds to remember me. She laughs, revealing a row of false front teeth fastened at the corners with a gold brace. She sweeps two woollen sweaters off over her head, hanging them on a hook. Then she takes hold of her hair and plaits it. She pulls a rubber band from her wrist and wraps it around the end of her braid, rolls up her loose blue trousers at the ankles, plucks her sports top into shape.

A few minutes later we're standing in the hall. The men interrupt their exercises and sit down on the floor. Wang's daughter walks over to a footstool under the windowsill. It's covered by a colourful cloth and positioned in front of a picture pinned to the wall, but I can't make out the intricate motif. On the stool are a pot containing incense sticks and a plate of fruit. Wang's daughter straightens the plate and plucks at the cloth, arranging the incense sticks anew. Then she sits down next to the fat boy in the waistcoat.

Her mother steps over to the long wall. My eyes, following her, fall upon an extensive collection of weapons attached to the wall. Staffs arranged by size rest on iron hooks. Above them, various blades hang on red woven tassels knotted around their shafts. There's a pair of crossed short sabres and a long, narrow sword that consists on closer inspection of two separate blades joined into one. Wooden swords, lances with silver-lacquered halberds, round batons joined by metal links and chain whips rolled up like snails are fastened with nails.

Wang takes a medium-sized staff, walks into the middle of the room and positions herself in front of us. She raises her left arm, balls her fist against the open right hand before her chest and stands before us in greeting.

Now she moves the staff to her centre, stretches her arms up and jumps, one leg bent, the other outstretched, into a deep squat. She swings the wood behind her head. She remains motionless like this, her face concentrated and expressionless, with eyes that seem to express something we can't recognize. Then she slides up again. She takes the stick by one end and runs, a sequence of steps around her own axis, swinging the weapon along with her. She turns at the window and falls back into the low position akin to half of a drawn bow, the staff stretched as far up as it will go and held behind her, herself as motionless as her weapon. Again she leaps up, her stick beating a series of blows at the air. She launches a jump-kick and turns around, whirling the stick in a figure-of-eight rotation. Once again, she glides into a low-drawn bow, suddenly throwing her head up, prising her lips open and smiling at me. Now her staff becomes a scythe. It slices the air in broad circles, up close to the audience's heads. Twice, Wang interrupts the scythe's circles, jumping down, slamming her weapon down horizontally on the floor before she launches it into motion again. Then she stretches, stands up again, stands to the left of the upright pole and places her hands against her chest in greeting as before.

I'm still standing at the door in my cardigan. I'm half in the doorframe, behind the desk sown with papers. My right foot is across the threshold, the left behind it. I've pulled my shoulders up, my elbows pressed to my ribs, my toes curled in my socks.

I'm standing the way little children do when their shoes are too small.

My hands are clenched into fists in my pockets. Not the way fighters do—the way helpless people do: four fingers hugging the thumbs.

18

März doesn't reach for the hand I've placed on his shoulder until just before we get off the tram. He turns it over, lays his damp forehead against it, raises his head and fishes for a pack of wilted paper tissues, their tips peeking out of the front pocket of his backpack. I press the stop button as the tram crosses the pedestrian subway back to the station. We get off.

März fetches us coffee and fries doused in ketchup at the first snack van. He eats greedily, sniffing occasionally. His elbows pressed against the plastic circle of a tabletop mounted on an empty barrel, he chews with his cheeks filled, tired and silent, subdued by his tears.

I shove my portion across the table to him, nibbling at the grooved edge of my plastic cup and watching him eat everything up. He throws the cardboard plates in the garbage sack under the tabletop and gets out his tobacco. I eye him as he rolls a cigarette, taps it down and lights it. I step from one foot to the other and wait for März to take his first drag, exhaling again with relief.

'It's my turn now. Tell me where you're meeting him.'

He pulls a face, runs the hand holding his cigarette over his head in an evasive gesture, and gives me a still watery, rather offended look.

'I have to call him first.'

'You mean we can choose where to meet him?'

März shrugs.

He crumples his empty cup, letting it snap back into its old shape, smoulders a hole in the plastic with the tip of his cigarette, takes a last draw and drops the butt into the cup. Then he turns around, dragging his backpack across the asphalt by a strap toward the station, up the smooth surface of a wheelchair ramp and into the hall.

I follow him at two paces' distance to the first telephone box. März goes in, rummages for change in his pockets and turns back to me. I walk up to the door, going to open it before I see too late that the glass has been smashed and removed, and tear open the inside of my right hand on a few remaining splinters of glass.

März has turned away again; he inserts a five-mark piece in the slot, wedges the receiver against his shoulder, dials and lets it ring for a long time.

'*C'est moi . . . oui . . . non . . . Ça dépend.*'

I give my hand a vigorous shake. Blood drips onto the metal window frame.

'Schöneweide . . . non, Schöneweide . . . c'est loin? . . . oui, je sais . . . c'est une maison? . . . d'accord . . . à bientôt.'

März hangs up, sees my bleeding hand, bends down and takes out the next tissue.

'Well . . . ?'

'An abandoned tourist cafe at Plänterwald. We're meeting in the woods behind it, in two hours.'

The park is exhausted from the winter.

We walk along the water, our eyes fixed to the gravel path, turned away from the bare trees, the washed-out, trampled grass fields spreading out wide ahead of us and verging on the river with no embankment to divide them from the water. Waterfowl hop along the benches, loitering at empty waste baskets, crossing the path close before our feet in hectic, hungry dashes.

März is talking. He tells me about a rap band from near Bad Homburg, a band I've never heard of. I try to let the words' meaning bounce off me, just taking in the sounds.

It's a long way. I feel weak; I ought to have eaten something. Breathing in presses the pipes in my chest pocket against my ribs. I wonder how long we've been walking; we'll probably turn up too late and miss the man.

We come across an ornate white building with stairs to the entrance, a beer garden and sales kiosks. Garlands of light bulbs, disconnected, are draped across folded tables. The kiosks are closed up, the chairs stacked and secured with chains. Behind them comes the arched bridge, the island, the pedal-boat hire. Skiffs lounge on the banks, abandoned over the winter, packed in protective sheeting covered with puddles. A boatless sheet hangs ragged and twisted from a mooring pole.

März has gone a few paces ahead. His index finger runs along the wet barrier, sending splashes of rain down the embankment. He's in a rush now, turning around to me several times. The distance between us increases. Now he's vanished behind the bridge.

I run after him. März has already reached the area behind the island. The park blends into the woods here, trees and bushes growing denser. Our path still takes us along the water. The fence around the fairground begins on the land side, a barrier wrapped in rotting basketwork, dampened screams penetrating from the other side, music, the grinding and rattling of the rides. I catch März up parallel to the big wheel.

'Are we too late?'

'Don't think so.'

'Why are you running then?'

'I want to get there earlier. Compose myself a bit, have a think. Plan what to say. I haven't seen him for more than ten years.'

'So he has no idea that you . . . ?'

'No. But that's not the problem.'

We come to a remote corner of the amusement park. The noise of the rides has stopped, a thinner growth of trees revealing a view of a pile of carousel cars waiting for repair, an imitation-rock slide stored on its side and the terminus of a narrow-gauge railway. In the far corner, just before the end of the fence, is a roller coaster put out to storage, dark red, egg-shaped cars stuck fast forever in the curves of a tower of rusted, steeply convoluted struts.

März stops. He points toward a small brick house, single-storey, double-winged, surrounded by shrubbery. An abandoned cafe; the old tourist place. Behind the shards of windowpanes, tables and chairs are still set up in an indication of their earlier arrangement.

März pulls a watch without a strap out of his jacket pocket.

'Still time.'

He puts the watch away again and goes over to the water. There's a wooden bench on the bank. We sit down. My head aches, my back shivers; the relief of sitting down seizes hold in the form of weakness and tiredness. März is squatting absently beside me, his knees drawn up and his hood over his head. He has pulled his zip up almost to his nose.

'You used to love her, back then, didn't you?'

'Who?' asks März—a superfluous question.

I rest my chin on my fists and fix my gaze on the cement works' silos on the opposite bank, two pencil-grey reactor-shaped blocks growing darker in the dwindling light. März sighs. He leans forward, takes out a penknife, jabs it into the wooden armrest and pulls it back out.

'We were in the same class for two years. When we were twelve and thirteen. We used to walk home from school together—we threw our leftover sandwiches off a bridge onto the roofs of passing cars. Sometimes we hung out in the park. We went sledging together, along the iced-up paths on the hill. We found the sledge in a hollow oak tree. All winter long, we sat inside that tree every afternoon. Sometimes just us, sometimes with other kids. We smoked cigarettes we stole from our parents. We played wink murder and spin the bottle, and when the bottle pointed to us we kissed with our lips pressed together.'

'And what you wrote . . . in the poetry album?'

März gives me a tortured look and digs away at the bench; rapid, angry stabs that pierce the wood as tick-shaped notches.

'And then last week I run into her at that market. She hasn't changed a bit—she's still just as thin and gawky as she used to be. Only her hair's longer—it used to be short like a boy's.'

He laughs, folds out the corkscrew on his penknife, jabs the point of the screw into one of the holes but it slips out, scraping his thumb. He curses, then starts screwing again. From time to time he blows shavings

out of the wood. The hole expands into a white hollow.
He leaves it be, notching out the next hole and another.
März spits, jabs and stirs with his blade, covering the
armrest with a palm-sized wound of sticky, scaly scabs
in the wood.

I turn away. Wind blows over the water across my
head. The surface of the river is smooth, reflecting the
dusk as it sets in. A small ferry illuminated yellow on the
inside casts off slightly further southeast of us, cruising
diagonally across to the mooring on the opposite bank. As
it crosses the middle of the river its waves reach us, curly
chains of motion washing up an orange drink carton.

I have to concentrate. I mustn't forget why I'm here.

In my jacket pocket, inside my fist, the cut from the
broken glass is stinging. I wait for the waves to smooth
out, trying to imagine the river flowing in its own and
the opposite direction at the same time.

The scratching and scraping of März's knife qui-
etens down and finally stops altogether. The hideous
face I always wanted to forget appears before my eyes,
forming out of river and memory.

A stubble of hair, a rampart of tangled silver-glitter-
ing earrings on a head much too large for his slim shoulders, like that of an embryo. A short nose covered in
grey freckles. Eyes with no colour, nicotine craters on
his cheeks. I start. A dog barks not far from here. The
hysterical yelping of a large breed, angry and over-
wrought. The sort of barking that makes you nervous,

when you never quite know whether the dogs are greeting someone or want to attack them.

März has gone.

With a leap, I'm on my feet and running to the brick building. I run up the steps to the entrance and stand on a veranda strewn with splintered tiles, dishevelled tufts of grass growing through the cracks. I rattle at the door handle. It's locked. I lower my head over the shards of windowpanes. The interior is dusty and empty. I walk back down the stairs and round the house. Against its rear wall is an empty dog kennel, a roll of corrugated iron, a cement machine, a heap of paving stones, gardening equipment.

März is nowhere to be seen.

The trees set in behind the house, a thinly spread mix of species threaded through with well-trodden paths. I break into a jog. Torn up and down by the rhythm of my legs striding, pushing off and then striding again, my gaze darts between the bare branches of birches, beeches and horse chestnuts. It catches on dead bushes, is torn onward, faces the sky now palpably sucking in the light as my head jerks upward to sling back sweat-sodden strands of hair, is directed back to the ground by a stumble over roots and branches, onto sparse undergrowth strewn with tin cans, crumpled tissues and dead leaves. Moments later I come across a wide path running parallel to the river, dividing the wood into two halves. I cross it, racing on, and spot lights. The headlights of cars driving past at close quarters flash through the branches.

Despairing, I come to a standstill and squat. I give a sob, take the pipe out of my pocket and chew at its mouthpiece. The crying abates. The bitter taste draws saliva into my mouth, which I spit out several times. I stand up again and run back toward the river, this time in a diagonal line. I have to comb through the woods again, this time off the paths.

It's almost dark on the ground now and I make slow progress. After several minutes of hectic trudging, I tread in a hole in the ground, twisting my left foot. As I'm still struggling on, pain stabs at my ankle and forces me to stop. I shake my leg, trying to turn the joint. I manage but it hurts. I put my foot on a sawn-off tree trunk, take long deep breaths and press the thumb and forefinger of my right hand against a point between two knuckles on my left. The pain in my hand superimposes that in my foot, migrating into my ankle as a pulsing sensation, switching off the other pain.

Voices, rustling leaves, crackling.

The fluorescent side stripes of tracksuits emerge from the undergrowth. Two young men and a girl are wandering along the path ahead of me, laughing. They sit down on a bench and lower their shorn heads over a plastic bag.

Taking cautious backward steps, I swerve off to a parallel path. From here, I reach the broad main path again. I stop and lean against one of the piles of tree trunks stripped of their bark and set up at short intervals by the side of the path. I can hear the teenagers still laughing, and I bore my knuckles into my temples to fill the sudden emptiness spreading inside me.

A shadow separates off from one of the woodpiles, not even twenty yards away. I can make out legs feeling their way ahead, a head emerging from the undergrowth, then come the body, shoulders and back.

I duck. Behind the first shadow, a second emerges. It's slim and agile, has a large head and is five foot three at most. Then comes the dog. The dog confuses me. A long-haired beast with a tail dragging on the floor, shrouded in curly fur. It's not the right race but that doesn't mean much; one dog year equals seven human years.

The three figures cross the path and duck back into the darkness of the trees, directly into the section of wood I've just come from. I leave the protection of the log pile, walking some twenty yards along the path to reach the point where I last saw them. A crooked path winds into the wood, ending at a seat made of halved tree trunks. By the time I've reached the bench I see that the trees thin out on my left, and I make out a patch of grass with see-saws and climbing frames made of brown-painted logs.

They're sitting on a wooden train. März on the engine, perched back on the boiler, his feet stretched up to the miniature driver's cab. The other man has sat down cross-legged on the roof of a carriage. His dog lies next to him and the backpack between the two of them, in a freight wagon filled with sand.

If I want to feel my way close enough, I'll have to walk around the playground under the shelter of the trees until I reach the place where they're sitting. I take a few steps back onto the path, head in the opposite direction until I feel far enough away, then I break into a run.

Zigzagging around the tree trunks, I don't let the two figures out of my sight. My breathing is noisy, my legs trample, the twigs beneath my feet cracking too loudly. Neither of the two men notices me. Only the dog has raised his head, pricking up his ears.

I creep up to two nearby trees. März is restless. He drums his thumb and ring finger against one knee at manic speed. I can only see the man opposite him from behind. He's sitting upright, legs still crossed, his hands resting on his thighs.

He shakes his head.

'*C'est pas vrai.*'

März says nothing, his drumming intensifying.

'*C'est pas vrai,*' the man repeats, looking at the backpack. The dog has stood up and starts walking around the engine with a growl in his throat. His master pats him on the back and pulls him closer by his collar, whispering in his ears and stroking them. The dog whines and sits back down.

'The woman . . .' März begins, inserting a cigarette between his lips.

'*Quelle femme . . . ?*' the man interrupts him.

'. . . The one I told you about . . .'

März pulls his lighter out of his pocket. I push past the sides of the pine trees. I have to see the man. I have to see his face when the flame comes.

'. . . You know . . .'

März rotates the flint wheel, sending up sparks. He curses, shakes the gas and adjusts the flame.

'. . . The one with the pouch and the two pipes . . .'

'*Je m'en fous,*' says the man; I'm turning away now.

'*Ça fait cinq ans que je ne fume plus.*'

19

I return the next day.

'Four weeks' preparation before you start training,' the small man in the ribbed shirt told me as he escorted me to the door. 'Two hours every day, whenever you have time. For a month. If you miss a day you're out. Think about it. You can start any time, but if you do start you have to keep it up. All you have to do is try your best.'

I'm outside the hall the next morning, clutching a cloth bag containing trainers and tracksuit pants. The entrance is open, the shoe shelf empty. The room is smaller than I recall. Next to the plate of fruit and the incense sticks is a vase of fresh flowers. Sunlight reveals the dirt on unwashed windows. A row of mats is laid out along the windowless long wall.

Hesitating, I walk toward the room at the end of the hall. Through a gap in the door I can see that the beds are folded out. The covers are still rumpled from the last sleep; quilts with threadbare patterns. There's a breakfast tray on the desk. I see a jar of jam, an empty breadbasket, two chipped mugs bearing the emblem of the local football team. Undecided, I stay put but don't dare to knock. I sit down on the mats and wait.

The man from yesterday enters the hall, slipping off flat black shoes at the entrance. As he does so, he looks at my buttoned boots with their worn heels. He smiles and goes to open a window.

'You can change right here,' he calls, not looking over at me.

I shake my sports clothes out of the bag. The man has gone out to the yard with a jug in his hand. I take off my jeans and cardigan and pull on a pair of sweatpants. He comes back and turns to the window, again not looking at me.

'Twenty minutes' warm-up run.'

He starts watering the pot plants on the windowsills.

The first laps are easy. Along the row of mats to the windows, past the entrance — still open — to the weapons on the long wall, to the changing room and back past the mats again. Next lap.

After three laps I'm feeling warm, after the fourth I start sweating. Real sweat, not saline ice water on goosepimples. Steaming vapour that exits not only from my armpits, but from all the pores on my body, wetting my hairline warm and making my fingers swell. Sweat runs down my forehead into my eyes and from my neck to my shoulders, pooling at the base of my spine and the backs of my knees. Sweat for which the speed of my pace becomes a cooling wind after the fourth and fifth lap, refreshing my entire body.

Then the euphoria's over. My new sneakers are rubbing my heels, one shoelace is coming loose. Five minutes have passed at most. At the very most. The man is still busy with the plants at the windows. He waters them with great deliberation. They're all yucca plants. Most of them are crooked and not very large, with long trunks in the middle fuzzy with the remains of dropped leaves and a few large leaves at the top.

I stop to tie my shoelace.

'Don't stop,' the man calls, turning around to me.

I give a start, tie a hasty knot in the half-fastened bow and carry on jogging again, but my legs refuse to cooperate. The elastic rubs around my midriff. Every step whips my ponytail against my damp neck. I slow down.

'Walk one lap if you can't run any more. Walk fast.' Now the man begins picking off dead leaves, blowing away dust here and there. He eyes the leaves, turning some of the pots around to the sunlight.

I walk. Walking is a relief. The lap is over far too quickly, but running seems easier again after that. The man leaves the room, this time with two jugs. I jog, walk, jog. The sweat dries and comes back at the same time. Dazed and with blistered heels, I drag myself around the room in a fug of bodily vapours. He comes back in the end, puts his jugs in the corner with the weapons and summons me over.

I pant, standing still.

He pulls me into the centre of the hall, positions himself in front of me and begins to rotate his arms. So I rotate my arms. He circles his hips. My hips circle. He bends and rotates his knees. My knees fold in and return upward in two obtuse circles. Ten times, then in the opposite direction. He does press-ups on his fists. I drop down to the floor, holding my weight on the palms of my hands. The smell of old parquet flooring stings my nose. As I lower my body my arms collapse. I fall, drag myself back up, try a second time. At twelve I give up and crawl to the mats, my head lowered.

The man walks over to me. He helps me to stand up again. He breathes in, showing me how his belly fills with air. I try to do the same but my breath goes between my ribs, my shoulders hunched. He smiles, taking my hand and holding it close to my body. I try to breathe against my hand. It works better. Now he stands opposite me, legs apart, lets his arms move slowly upward as he breathes in, pressing the palms of his hands back down again as he expels the air. We stand and breathe, high on oxygen that makes my head spin.

'Now we'll practice the bow position.'

The man places his hands on his hips, bends his front leg and stretches the other back, standing low. We walk along the long wall of the hall, keeping to the bow position, our hands on our hips, from the entrance to the changing room. Now and then I have to stop so he can correct me.

'Lower. Stretch your leg right out. Feet not too parallel.'

Now we walk the same length back. My thighs cramp up. The coach walks over to the wall, pulls a pole out of the stand and holds it over my head.

'No higher than this. Stay low while you walk forward.'

A door squeaks behind me.

'Mabu!' a piercing voice calls across the room.

The man waves me over, telling me to shake out my legs. Time for a break. I sit down on the mat. Wang nods at me from the doorway. The man has walked over to her and they're talking in low voices. I gaze out of the window, breathless, my knees burning.

Now Wang comes toward me. I get up. Wearing yesterday's blue pants and top, she positions herself opposite me. She's holding two empty buckets in her right hand. They're tin pails with handles and plastic grips, the kind used to store supplies in restaurant kitchens. She places them both on the floor in front of me, one in front of each foot. Then she fetches the water jugs. She places one jug in front of each bucket.

'Mabu,' she repeats.

'Horse position,' calls the man, busy with the fastenings of the punching bag to one side of us.

Wang stretches out her arms and touches both my shoulders until I'm standing exactly opposite her. She points at her feet and then her shoulders again. I'm to stand with my feet shoulder-width apart and then pull my feet apart in a zigzag three times, until our legs are wide. Wang squats low, her back straight. I imitate her. She gestures for me to stay still, jumps out of her position and corrects me.

'Drop your shoulders. Push your hips forward. Toes not parallel, pointing outward,' the man calls from behind us.

She looks at me, nodding.

I come back up. Wang pours a splash of water into each bucket. She picks them up and gestures at me. I bend my knees into the horse position like she showed me. She holds the buckets out to me. I grip one handle in each hand. The buckets are light. They're still light now. I test their weight in my hands and find it exactly equal; I can't tell the slightest difference.

I stand in the horse position, looking out of the window. The windowsills emit a scent of wet plants, mixed with dust. Water has seeped down through the earth and runs into the saucers beneath, thick yellowish drips of limescale hanging from their edges. The largest of the plants is perched on a soup bowl. It's on the brink of overflowing. The elastic edge of the overhanging water trembles slightly, bulging outwards. My thighs ache and I hear a fly buzzing, reeling to and fro between the tangle of leaves and the windowpane. It alights on the lowest leaf, rubbing its trembling front legs against one another. Then it tries again, reverberating from the windowpane and landing on the edge of the plate.

The surface tension breaks, the water spilling onto the window ledge, sweeping the fly along with it.

20

The dog howls out and makes a leap into the bushes. We're facing one another.

He fixes his eyes on me, pulling back the flaps of skin around his mouth with a throaty growl, exposing fangs and tensing the muscles of his back legs. I kick as he's in mid-leap. His rib cage crashes against the edge of my foot. He doubles up, landing on his side and thrashing his paws. He flashes me an offended look and whines.

I turn away and run toward the road, half twisted around and limping. I can see the man on the train out of the corner of my eye. He jumps up and bends over his dog. The dog gets back to his feet, shakes himself and starts barking hysterically, his snout turned in my direction.

'Where are you? Come back!'

März shouts into the trees but stays where he is, while the other man emits a series of incomprehensible curses and takes steps in my direction. My teeth clenched, I run a short way, find the main path, cross it and duck behind a grit container. I hear his footsteps crunching on the ground. Then he emerges from the undergrowth. Breathing heavily, my lips pressed against the metal arch of a padlock, I peer over the container's lid. I make out his head over the edge.

The man steps onto the path and looks around. I reach for the pressure point on my hand in the dark. He seems to be listening. The pressure on my hand hardly overpowers the pain in my foot any more. For a moment the man stands there listening, then he turns around and walks back into the woods.

I stay sitting on the ground for a while, turned around now, my eyes closed and my back leaning on the grit box. I hear the dog's barking in the distance, hear it getting quieter until it's moved away from me toward the river.

Rain sets in. Fine, almost frozen drops, running through the bare network of branches with a broad rushing sound. They gather on the branch above me in ribs of semi-peeled bark, falling onto my hair in splashes. The rain seeps through to my scalp, icing up my neck, numbing my disappointment and any feeling of time.

Night falls. A cat screeches in the playground. I push myself up, rubbing my stiff knees and stepping onto the path. I drag myself along for a while. A gnawed stick is resting against the post of a sign providing orientation for fairground visitors. I take it, lean on it and limp out of the woods.

The road is a dual carriageway, the traffic sparser now. Behind the living room windows of unadorned residential buildings grouped around car parks and unkempt patches of grass flicker the blue-green flames of televisions. I spot a bus stop for the 265 and walk up to the yellow post. The timetables have been torn out.

A taxi approaches from the east. I thrust one arm out to wave, the other dropping the stick. I search my pants and find the change from the bakery in the small front pocket on my right, crumpled green and brown notes wrapped around a few coins.

The driver stops. I open the back door of the car and he waits for me to get in. He cranes his neck at the mirror in mistrust. I say: 'Lehniner Strasse,' and close the door. The interior light goes out. He hears my voice, relaxes and presses a button on the meter.

Within minutes, the stumps of the plane trees on Puschkinallee have passed us by. We drive over large crossroads almost devoid of other vehicles. The rear of the car smells of air freshener, curry powder and cleaning fluid. We hit a run of yellow lights at the East Side Gallery, the driver braking at regular intervals. The taxi comes to a halt next to the post of a stop sign with an orange waste bin attached to it. I unfasten my seatbelt, reach into my jacket pocket and wind the window down. My arm extended out of the window up to my armpit, I touch the metal ring attaching the bin to the pole. I stretch, pushing a little section of my shoulder further out. My hand clutches a corner of the leather pouch and the mouthpieces of the pipes.

I feel for the opening of the container. The ritual is always the same: my grip turns to the grip on the buckets and Wang enters the room with full jugs. I pick up the buckets one last time, bending my knees. Wang pours the water. The metal ridges measure the water level; two ridges higher every time, and the marker pen line drawn at the upper third of the container has inched closer to the water level every day. Wang empties the jugs with full swing, the water dancing around the line. I keep up my position, looking out of the window as the tension grows in my thighs. I've accustomed myself to a stare that slices the two or three minutes of holding out into several horizontal sections, my eyes feeling their way across the row of windows.

I start at the very top, by the unused olive-green curtain tracks, glide along them from left to right and then back again, slightly lower, to the tilted upper panes, and on, to and fro and back, to the handles, the top leaves of the plants, and on until I end up at the very bottom by the window ledges, until Wang claps her hands.

But she doesn't clap her hands. Does she not clap today, or have I overheard her clapping? Is she standing behind me and waiting for me to turn around, so that she can close her fist and her open palm together as a farewell gesture, like every day? I can't bear the sight of the window ledge any longer. My arms and legs hurt so badly. I have to let go of my burden. Whatever happens, I have to let go of my burden.

Now open your hand. Throw down the weight. Pull your arm in.

The man at the steering wheel looks around at me, perturbed.

Shivering, he raises his shoulders, shifts to first gear and puts his foot down.

'Everybody's giving up smoking,' he grumbles as we accelerate, shaking his greying hair styled into curls at the back of his neck, leaning forward and lighting a Gitanes Maïs.

Later he turns on the radio. Interrupted by crackling radio messages, he presses the buttons for various stations, curses and removes a CD from its case. Classical highlights, performed by a Japanese symphony orchestra.

At Rosa-Luxemburg-Platz I tug a fifty-mark note out of my pocket, squint at the meter and see that a twenty would do. We turn onto my street. I point at Number Fourteen; the driver brakes and presses the meter button and I pass him the note.

And then I'm standing outside my house.

The front door is open. Why is the front door open? I can see through to the yard from here, standing on the road.

Shock takes hold of me, cold as shivers. The taxi makes a U-turn behind me. For a moment I long to be back in the car, long for the warm fug of the heater, the sounds of the Bohemian Fields to the scent of yellow-rolled cigarettes, for a soft-suspended, soundless and thoughtless drive through the night.

The driver revs his engine and drives off toward Wilhelm-Pieck-Strasse.

Hesitating, I set my foot in the entrance. The yard is heaped with junk. In the middle is a large skip, almost blocking the way to the side building. A few windows are wide open, slamming against each other at irregular intervals. Slats of wood are leant against the carpet-beating frame, behind them a refrigerator, jammed between old kitchen cupboards. The cream upholstered suite from the ground floor has been heaved over a window ledge. Vertical, its legs outstretched, it now stands by the stairs to the basement.

I raise my head to the fourth floor. Everything on the fourth floor is closed and quiet.

Later. It's dark in my room.

I'm lying in bed, my eyes closed; my other senses refuse to switch off. Creaking floorboards, the palms of my hands on the cold bedcover, car doors slamming, an ankle swollen warm. Thirst, strong enough to keep me awake but not strong enough to limp across the floor-boards to the tap in the kitchen. Now and then a smoth-ered rumbling sounds out through the stove doors. A semi-smouldered tower of briquettes has collapsed, small sections subsiding through the fist-sized hole in the now concave grating into the ash drawer.

No, it's not a state of waking any more; it's a transi-tion, this semi-dozing. My eyelids won't open any more, even though my eyeballs are thrashing around to get free. They roll from left to right, from top to bottom, ever more urgent, ever faster, sketching flashing circles into my visuals.

After a while the circles round into heads.

Two men's heads, flaring up, dissolving into blind-ness and flaring up again. The picture, which I recognize more clearly with every flash of light, shows a backyard under snow. The snow is porous, the colour of burnt-out disposable camera flashes. The kind you put on cheap cameras next to the shutter release. On the ground, a concrete surface sealed with tar seams, next to a pallet of piled empty lettuce crates and tin pails filled with ran-cid fat, are two men. They're lying directly below the window of a restaurant kitchen, a clatter of pans and plates emanating from within.

A weak light shines out of the kitchen window, highlighting the men's contours at protruding points but not illuminating them entirely. Their eyes wide open and their legs half splayed, they're lying on their backs. Their heads are touching and their fists are clenched, one each next to a shoulder and one on their bellies. The men's jackets aren't fastened; you can see the waxy-white sections of skin on their necks and chests. One of the two has dark hair and the shadow of a beard. Embedded in remainders of vomit, his tongue lolls out of the corner of his mouth. The other man is blond. He has a cut in his neck surrounded by dried blood, and between the hairs on his semi-exposed chest is the empty tube of a pen.

I take a step closer.

Only a few steps, but the two men look much younger close up. Two slim bodies in snowsuits, strewn with leftover food and vegetable peelings. They're wearing bobble hats, the blond one even has mittens on, and the dark man's face isn't stubbly—it's dirt smeared around his chin.

My eyes fall on his hand.

It's lying on his chest, next to the half-open zip, a hand with tiny fingers frozen stiff, intertwined with the remains of a sledge string.

21

I wake up. Somebody's knocking, a low persistent knock with a single knuckle. I push aside sweat-moistened pillows, roll myself off the mat and test my weight on my ankle. The swelling's gone down.

My pulse revved, panicking from the unfamiliar knocking sound, I run along the hall. I never have visitors. I can't even remember the sound of the doorbell. Breathing heavily, I press down the handle and pull the door open, just a hand's width. I look outside, my mouth opening.

Dunkel is in the corridor.

She's standing there in a long wrap-around skirt embroidered with birds perched on cherry-blossom branches with their beaks ajar. She's tied the tips of an angora cardigan reaching just under her ribs in a knot over her stomach. One hand on her hip, the other hand, decorated with eight to twelve thin silver bangles, leaning against my doorframe.

'Hi, firewoman,' she hums. Her voice is much lower than I'd have thought. 'Come over when you've woken up, I'll invite you round for breakfast.'

She smiles at me, waiting for an answer. She looks good. She's never looked as good as this. I'm still standing in the gap in the doorway, holding my sweaty face creased by sleep out into the hall and not managing to make a sound. In the end I nod. She turns on her heel and goes back into her flat. I nod again at her back and close the door behind her.

Ten minutes later, I've run several litres of cold water over my face and combed my hair, knotted into cherry-sized nests at the back of my head, for the first time in days. I've scrubbed my fingernails with a brush, failed to find a clean pair of pants but located a black sweater with no stains on it and a blackened silver chain with a moonstone in the centre. I spit on a tissue, wipe the forest earth from my shoes, then I search the kitchen for something edible. To no avail. Empty-handed, I'm soon standing outside the opposite flat.

The door's ajar. I walk in.

Dunkel is standing in her room. The room is full of cardboard boxes. She stalks around the boxes with a strained face, throwing objects into them or turning them over indecisively in her hands, looking at the content of the boxes, only to throw them onto a large heap piled up close to the window, a heap of full ring binders, tins, crumpled clothing and soot-stained kitchen appliances. After a while she notices me and waves me in with a distracted smile.

First I go into the kitchen. The shelves have been partly cleared, the cooker pushed out from the wall, on the table is another cardboard box—not a trace of breakfast. I leave the kitchen and walk into Dunkel's room. She's standing at her desk, running both hands through her hair, plucking at a strand, twirling it, and then she sticks it between her lips and then behind her ear.

'No point in tidying up this mess!' she shouts. 'The stuff I want to take with me goes in the boxes. I'll leave the rest here. Let them throw all the junk out the window!'

'You mean you're moving out?'

'Aren't you?' She gives me a confused look.

Suddenly I remember the letter. I turn around, run back into the corridor and into my flat. My anorak is on the floor next to my bed. It's still damp from yesterday. I reach into the breast pocket. The letter's still there. The paper feels clammy and soft but it's unharmed. I tug it out of the pocket and stroke it smooth, holding it to my chest and talking it back to Dunkel's room.

She sees me coming in and I hold the letter out to her. Her eyes alight on the envelope with the blue house, then on the translucent window with her name in it. She raises her eyebrows in surprise.

'I found it on your kitchen table. I thought it might be important for you, or for us . . . I didn't know . . . You weren't here.'

I feel myself blushing. Dunkel seems to want to reply but thinks better of it at the last moment. She sighs, takes the envelope and throws it in the nearest box.

'Can you help me? I have to pull the desk away from the wall.' Each of us grabs hold of one end, turning it slightly and pushing it into the middle of the room. Dunkel sweeps objects off the desktop with both hands. Coins rain down on the floorboards, the tin falls off the edge and gets caught in the cactus. Papers sail after it, a folder bangs into half-open drawers. Dunkel sighs, laughs and sighs again, swinging herself onto the desktop, dangling her legs and resting her chin on her hands.

'We ought to get out of here now. There's that cafe round the corner. You know the one.'

Her hands leave her chin, slide over her thighs, pluck at her skirt and reach the edge of the desk.

'The Romanian guy's place. They do breakfast there too.'

She smiles at me. She runs her forefinger along the edge, looking for the place and finding it. M.M. Her fingertip dabs along the jagged letters, tracing the curves by touch, her face still smiling and waiting for my answer.

I nod. Dunkel leaps off the desk and over to the bed, fishes a coat-sized woollen shawl from the bedpost and wraps herself up in it.

It's not raining any more but the junk in the yard is still dripping and the air is cold and damp. We squeeze past the skip. Dunkel kicks aside a ball of furniture stuffing. We clamber over two legless bedside tables and an empty toolbox and reach the exit. The front corridor still smells strongly of urine. She holds her nose until we get to the street.

Outside she takes my arm, as if she had to lead the way. She's got new shoes, ankle-boots with zips and platform soles that make her look at least six inches taller. Shivering, she pulls the shawl tighter around her shoulders. Her walking leaves clacking sounds on the cobbles.

'That letter was an old one,' she explains, her eyes fixed on the road. 'They sent it the month before last. They offered me a replacement flat. Two rooms, three streets away from here.'

We turn onto Weinbergsweg. Dunkel stumbles on a crack in the paving stones, her ankle caving in, but she regains her balance. What ridiculous shoes. We walk past the bakery, the scent of oven heat and fresh rolls wafting out at us. The shop assistant with the diamond stud in her temple is standing in the doorway, pale with her apron drooping. She bends down for a roll of tape and hangs a poster of icing-sugared jam doughnuts in the window.

Dunkel's pace picks up. She walks two feet ahead, pulling me after her by the arm. She pushes the door to Mirca's cafe open with a jerk, letting her shawl slip off her shoulders and hanging it on one of the pointed hooks. Now she gestures with her hand flat, encouraging me to do the same and attach my anorak to one of the metal strands. I shake my head, keeping my jacket on my arm.

Dunkel strides between the seats to my regular table but thinks better of it at the last moment. She chooses a seat in the niche opposite. We sit down. The cafe is empty but for the tired hipster sitting at the window again today, drinking milk with honey and staring outside, her face expressionless.

Mirca comes out of the kitchen. He heads behind the bar but then notices us, doubling back to our table. He greets Dunkel with a slight smile. His eyes glide over me without a sign of recognition.

Dunkel orders two champagne breakfasts. She leans back in her seat, twisting her bangles and seemingly waiting for me to say something.

Behind the bar, chair-legs are shoved into place with a clatter. Mirca's son has climbed onto a barstool. He takes a cardboard coaster out of a stand and puts a glass of Coke down on it. Then he picks up the glass again, drinks several sips, slides the coaster aside a little and puts the drink down again. His index finger draws circles in the wet spot that the dripping glass has left behind on the surface of the counter.

His father is standing next to him, pouring sparkling wine into tall glasses. He puts them on a small oval wooden tray and brings them over to our table. Dunkel and I raise our glasses. We move them slightly closer together but don't clink them, and then we take our first sips.

Mirca's son has turned around and is now sitting with his back to the cafe. He leans forward and switches on the computer against the wall behind the bar, above the spirits bottles on the lowest of the mirrored shelves. The screen lights up.

On the way to the kitchen, Mirca looks over at his son and smiles. The boy presses a couple of buttons, the opening screen disappears and a coordinates system of little numbered and lettered boxes builds up.

I turn the glass in my hand. Bubbles form at the edges. They grow larger, writhing, tearing loose with a jerk and racing to the surface.

I put the glass to my lips.

I'm going to drink it in one. When it's empty I'm going to put it down on the table in front of me. Then I'm going to take a deep breath, stretch my nose and chin out to Dunkel and ask if she needs someone to share her new flat.